More than Neighbors

SHANNON STACEY

HARLEQUIN

SPECIAL
EDITION

HARLEQUIN®
SPECIAL EDITION™

Recycling programs for this product may not exist in your area.

ISBN-13: 978-1-335-89469-4

More than Neighbors

Harlequin Enterprises ULC
22 Adelaide St. West, 40th Floor
Toronto, Ontario M5H 4E3, Canada
www.Harlequin.com

Printed in U.S.A.

A *New York Times* and *USA TODAY* bestselling author of over forty romances, **Shannon Stacey** grew up military and lived many places before landing in the small New Hampshire town where she has resided with her husband and two sons for over twenty years. Her favorite activities are reading and writing with her dogs at her side. She also loves coffee, Boston sports and watching too much TV. You can learn more about her books at www.shannonstacey.com.

Books by Shannon Stacey

Carina Press

Boston Fire

Heat Exchange
Controlled Burn
Fully Ignited
Hot Response
Under Control
Flare Up

The Kowalski Series

Exclusively Yours
Undeniably Yours
Yours to Keep
All He Ever Needed
All He Ever Desired

Visit the Author Profile page
at Harlequin.com for more titles.

For my husband and sons, and for J and AJ. There are many people in my life I'm thankful for, but without the five of you, this dream probably wouldn't have come true.

Chapter One

"Is that our new house, Mommy?"

Meredith Price might have sat in her sporty SUV, strangling the steering wheel with white-knuckled fingers, until the sun went down if not for the tiny voice from the back seat.

"Yes, honey." She killed the engine and un-fastened her seat belt. Knowing that was the signal they were getting out of the car, the small white dog that had been napping next to Sophie leaped between the seats and into her lap.

"It's small."

Meredith hadn't done the math, but she was pretty sure their new home was smaller than the garage area of the six-thousand-square-foot home they'd left behind. "It's the perfect size for the two of us."

Oscar yipped, as if to remind her there were three members of the Price family, and she tried to keep the fluffy bichon frise still long enough to clip his leash onto his collar. "Be still, Oscar."

"I want to get out," her daughter whined.

"Hold on a second, Sophie. We can't open the doors until Oscar's leash is on." She heard the frustration in her voice and took a long, slow breath. "Wait for me to open your door, okay?"

She couldn't blame either of them for being anxious to get out of the car. The road trip from California to New Hampshire had been too much for a six-year-old and an energetic dog, even with more stops than Meredith had planned for.

Flying out and paying to have the car shipped probably would have made more sense, but driving cross-country had seemed like a grand adventure at the time. It had been an adventure, all right, though *grand* probably wasn't the word she'd use for it.

Once she'd managed to get Oscar on the leash, she stepped out of the car and set the little dog on the ground. He immediately sprinted to the grass and lifted his leg, and Meredith heard the car door slam as Sophie got out. Within seconds, her daughter's hand was tucked in hers as they both stared at their new home.

"What's wrong, Mommy?"

Forcing her expression to relax into a smile, she looked down at the sweet face that was a younger version of her own. They had the same long, thick dark blond hair and oval faces with noses that were just a little too small. "Nothing, honey. I'm just tired because that was a very long drive."

"You look scared."

"I'm not scared, silly." She lied to her daughter because it was easier than admitting the truth.

Scared might be a strong word, but the anxiety and doubt that had been her constant companion since leaving San Diego only intensified as they walked to the front door.

The home she'd bought from three thousand miles away based on nothing but a video tour, her gut instinct and hazy, warm memories of growing up happy in Blackberry Bay, New Hampshire.

She punched the code the real estate agent had given her into the keypad next to the door. When the lock disengaged, she took another deep breath—they never really helped—and turned the handle.

Sophie bolted inside and, as soon as the door was closed and Meredith unclipped his leash, Oscar scrambled after her.

Meredith leaned against the closed door and breathed in the light scent of citrus, probably from whatever the cleaning service had used, and allowed herself to savor this moment.

This was the place she'd chosen to start over. Only four years old, the house was a small, single-story contemporary that was totally open concept except for the two bedrooms on the end, with a bathroom between them. The cream walls, hardwood floors and high-end finishes aligned perfectly with her taste, and because it was meant to be a summer get-away, it was furnished for comfort, with an over-stuffed sofa and chairs in a pale blue.

The previous owners hadn't wanted to deal with emptying out what had been a third home for them, so Meredith had been able to negotiate a turnkey price that included all the furnishings, right down to the comforters the owners had chosen to comple-ment the bedroom wall colors—though she'd brought new sheets with her. She'd had her hands full with the San Diego house and had been happy to avoid having to choose between picking out furniture for a house three thousand miles away or waiting until they arrived.

It hadn't been *all* practicality on her part, though. As soon as she'd clicked on the listing, she'd been interested in the house, but it was the interior shots that had her making an offer. The existing decor was all about peace and relaxation and light, and she'd fallen in love instantly.

It wouldn't be a summer getaway for her and Sophie, though. It would be their home, and judging from Sophie's excited chattering to Oscar, she'd chosen well.

"Wait," she called when she spotted her daughter reaching for the handle of the sliding door leading out to the deck. "Oscar needs to be on his leash before you open any doors."

Sophie was practically dancing in anticipation as she waited, and Meredith grinned at her before clipping Oscar's leash on and pulling open the sliding glass door. This was the most animated she'd seen her daughter since Devin had died in a car accident two years ago, leaving her without a husband and Sophie without her beloved Daddy.

Meredith took in the expanse of water before her and it felt like a healing balm for her soul. Blackberry Bay was an offshoot from Lake Winnipesaukee, and it was just the right size for lake life, without the big, fast boats. There was a canoe off to her left, and to the right she could make out a group of stand-up paddleboarders.

She mentally added buying a small paddleboat to her list of things to maybe do. Devin had left them more than comfortable, plus the sale of their home had bought this house and its furnishings with quite a lot left over, so it would be many years before she had to worry about money if she was smart. And part of being smart was establishing a budget, even if one wasn't technically necessary.

Eventually, once school had started and they were settled in, Meredith would figure out how she wanted to fill her days. She didn't *have* to work, but she knew by then she'd want to, plus it would leave the majority of their accounts and investments untouched, except for the bigger expenses. Lakefront properties came with hefty tax bills, for one thing.

But it was worth it. The deck was made of a composite material that looked like wood, but wouldn't splinter or peel. It spanned the width of the house and extended far enough out to have a patio set and a grill along with the built-in storage seating benches.

The stairs led down to the yard, which wasn't big, but it had beautiful grass and sloped gently to a short strip of sand at the water's edge. A wooden dock extended out into the lake, and at the end was a covered swinging love seat. Wildflowers had been planted around the dock, which Meredith hadn't noticed in the photos and videos from the real estate agent.

As surprises in buying a house sight unseen went, unexpected flowers were definitely a good one.

"Be careful," she called to Sophie, who had picked Oscar up and walked onto the dock.

Her daughter was a good swimmer, but the dog wasn't. And now that they'd be living on the water instead of visiting it, they'd have to have a serious discussion about water safety.

"Who are you?" she heard Sophie ask, and Meredith's head jerked up from the flower bed she'd been bent over.

A man was standing in the next yard, and he startled her enough so she didn't chide Sophie for being rude. It was a valid question.

"I'm Cam," he said in a deep voice that matched his outside. He was tall and broad shouldered, with dark hair and the kind of scruffy jaw that said the beard wasn't deliberate, but more a result of not bothering to shave for a few days. And, while he was wearing jeans and loafers, he wasn't wearing a shirt. Judging by the pinkish cast to his light tan, shirtless wasn't his usual state of attire. "Who are you?"

"Sophie. This is my new house. And this is my dog. His name is Oscar."

"Hello," Meredith said, drawing the stranger's attention to her before Sophie could spill any more details.

"Hi." He looked at her, and he was close enough so she could see the bright blue of his eyes. "In keeping with the theme, who are *you*?"

"My name is Meredith. Are you…a groundskeeper of some sort?"

It seemed like a legitimate question—working outside might explain why he wasn't wearing a shirt when it wasn't even hot—so she was surprised when he laughed. And even more surprised when she caught herself smiling because he had a great laugh.

"I'm not the lawn guy. I'm staying here for the summer."

Meredith shook her head in confusion. "You're renting this cottage?"

Unlike the old cottages that had been torn down to make way for the newer, much more expensive models, the summer home next door was original. And very colorful, if a little shabby.

The old clapboard siding was painted a pale pink and the trim was turquoise. The crooked window boxes, some of which had plastic flowers and little whirligigs in them, offered pops of color. It was essentially the total opposite of Meredith's sleek, white cedar–sided contemporary.

"No, I'm not renting it. It's mine."

"The real estate agent told me Mrs. Archambault lived next door." Despite having only vague memories of the older woman, she had been one of the reasons Meredith had chosen this house over two others. She wanted Sophie to learn to bond with people, and a grandmotherly neighbor would have been a good start.

His expression closed off. "She doesn't live here anymore."

* * *

Cam Maguire wasn't sure what to make of finding a beautiful woman, a little girl and a tiny bit of fluff that he was pretty sure was a dog in the yard when he went outside to look for his grandmother's cat.

He'd heard all the jokes about cats being real jerks and secretly plotting the demise of the humans who cared for them. He used to laugh at those jokes.

He didn't laugh anymore.

"I don't understand," the woman—Meredith, she'd said her name was—said and he realized she was still confused about why he was living next door to her.

"The woman who lived here, Carolina Archambault, was my grandmother and she passed away recently. I guess it must have been after you talked to your real estate agent about the neighbors."

"I'm so sorry for your loss."

"Thank you," he said, because it was the right thing to say. And he did feel a sense of loss.

It was his loss that he'd never met the woman who was his biological paternal grandmother and who had lived in this eccentric and colorful cottage by the lake.

"There you are," he said to the extremely large and very long-haired black cat who sauntered into the yard as if she hadn't disappeared for four hours to who knew where. And she had burrs in her tail again. Getting those things out of her fur made him wish he'd been a hockey goalie in college so he'd have the proper safety equipment for the job. "I've been looking for you."

Elinor—which was a ridiculous name for a cat, if you asked him—ignored him as expected and walked onto the neighbor's grass as if she owned it.

The little girl had left the dock and was exploring the yard with her dog, its leash clutched in her little hand. The dog watched the cat warily, but appeared to be smart enough not to mess with her. And Sophie was a cute kid, with long brownish-blond hair like her mother's. They looked a lot alike, actually, right down to their serious expressions.

"I'd offer to give you tips on living in Blackberry Bay," he said, "but I haven't been here very long."

"I'm from here, actually. I've been in California for years, so it might have changed a little, but I'm guessing not very much."

"What brings you back?" He instantly regretted asking the question when sadness flitted across her pretty face and settled in the tautness of her mouth.

"My husband passed away a couple of years ago and I decided Sophie and I would be happier here, near my parents. And I have some pretty fond memories of the town, too."

As her words sank in, he looked back to the little girl, trying to imagine how devastating it must have been for her to lose her daddy at such a young age. And how much harder the grieving process must have been for Meredith because she had to get Sophie through it. He'd never suffered that kind of loss, but imagining their sorrow hit him in the gut.

"I'm sorry about your husband," he said sincerely as he looked back to Meredith.

"Thank you." She gave him a tight smile. "So you're staying for the summer, you said? Where do you usually live?"

"New York City, actually."

Her hazel eyes widened. "Wow. That's quite a change in pace."

"It is, but I was ready to get away for a while."

"What do you do in the city?"

"I work for my dad," he said, which wasn't technically a lie, but wasn't entirely accurate, either. "A lot of accounting and paperwork and boring stuff like that."

She was cute when she wrinkled her nose. "I'm not a fan of boring math-related paperwork."

A yelp from across the yard caught her attention and she turned to see Elinor swipe at the white puffball. Sophie was frowning and picked the dog up, turning her body so the cat couldn't see him anymore.

"Your cat appears to be bullying my dog."

"She's not my cat. And you're embarrassing your dog by even making that claim right now."

She arched an eyebrow at him. "If you don't think cats can bully dogs, you don't spend a lot of time on the internet."

"She just wants the dog to know who's boss, I guess."

"It's his yard," she pointed out.

"She's a cat."

"Point taken." A genuine smile lit up her face and made her eyes crinkle. "They'll get used to each other. And speaking of that, now that I know you're going to be my neighbor for a while, I should probably introduce myself properly. I'm Meredith Price, and that's Sophie and Oscar."

"Calvin Maguire," he said, extending his hand. "But everybody calls me Cam."

As she shook his hand, he noted how soft the skin was and had to resist rubbing his thumb over it.

She tilted her head as she smoothly pulled her hand away from his. "How do you get Cam from Calvin?"

"My initials. Calvin Anthony Maguire." His mouth twisted in a wry smile. "The fourth."

"Interesting."

"It was a better alternative than being Little Cal for my entire life." He didn't really want to open himself up to more questions about his family, since they were the last thing he wanted to talk about. "Since Oscar's from California, let me guess. Oscar de la Renta?"

She laughed. "Oscar the Grouch."

"You're kidding." He looked at the dog again, who looked like the kind they put on the packaging of fancy dog food. "I don't really see the resemblance, but maybe it's a personality thing."

"He's actually named after Sophie's favorite book at the time, and trust me, we spent days explaining to her why we couldn't make his hair green."

"He doesn't bark a lot, does he?"

"I wouldn't say he barks a lot." She glanced at the dog before giving him a sheepish look. "It's more like a really high-pitched yip."

"That'll be fun while I'm reading over spreadsheets," he said, picturing spending his summer being harassed by a stubborn cat and a high-strung dog. "Maybe I should have packed my noise-canceling headphones."

She looked startled for a second and then her eyes narrowed. "I have a child and a dog, so I guess you'll just have to figure out how to make it work."

"Maybe a muzzle?" he asked, but he wasn't really serious. Yipping dogs weren't his favorite, but he wasn't a total jerk.

She stared at him for a long moment before giving

him an arch look. "I don't know if I can find one in your size, but I can try."

Cam chuckled, appreciating her comeback, but she didn't even crack a smile. Maybe she hadn't been joking. And maybe she'd thought he wasn't, either.

"If you'll excuse me, we just arrived and I have a lot to do."

"Nice to meet you," he said as she walked, and she held up her hand in what looked more like a dismissive gesture than a wave.

That was fine. If she wanted to play that game, she'd find out he didn't really care that much. She and her yipping dog could stay in her yard and he'd stay in his.

He had better things to do, anyway. Like learning more about Carolina Archambault, and figuring out how to convince her cat he was the boss.

Chapter Two

"I'm definitely adding building a fence to my to-do list," Meredith told Oscar as she stood in the yard, waiting patiently for the dog to find just the perfect place to do his business.

Even though it was the middle of June, the morning was damp and chilly, and she regretted letting Oscar's potty dance push her into going outside with nothing but a light cardigan thrown over her sleep shorts, cami and flip-flops.

But it was a new yard and Oscar wanted to make sure he'd sniffed every blade of grass before deciding on a good spot, so Meredith clutched her cardigan closed with her free hand and shivered.

"We definitely need a fence," she said. "That way I can open the door and let you out, and you can take all the time you need."

"Moving in and putting up a fence first thing, huh?" A deep male voice—his voice—spoke, and Meredith whirled to face it, wrapping Oscar's leash around her legs.

Cam was standing on his back deck, thankfully wearing a shirt this time. The tight gray Henley did little to tone down his sex appeal, though, and she tried to ignore her growing awareness of just how little.

She hadn't dated since Devin passed away, and at times she wondered if she ever would again. So feeling this buzz of sexual awareness was new, and she wasn't entirely sure if it was welcome or not. It was a comfort to know she still had those feelings. But having them for Cam Maguire wasn't ideal.

On the one hand, it was fairly safe to be attracted to a man who'd be leaving at the end of the summer. It was temporary. But on the other hand, one summer could feel like a long time when trying to ignore a very sexy man she was undoubtedly going to see every day since he lived next door. She wanted to savor the hot flush of physical desire, but not act on it because she had enough on her plate already—she'd just moved all the way across the country and had a little girl to get settled. Resisting Cam would be a lot easier if he wasn't practically within arm's reach.

He was holding a massive pink ceramic mug with a cat paw etched onto it, and steam drifted away from the rim. "Fences don't seem very neighborly."

"Then you can be neighborly and stand over here with my dog while he takes his sweet time," she said, trying to ignore the fact she wasn't really dressed for a conversation with her new neighbor.

Actually, she wasn't really dressed to talk to anybody except her daughter and her dog, but especially not to the handsome guy next door. But when his gaze traveled down her legs before returning to her face, she lifted her chin and refused to feel embarrassed.

Hey, she had great legs.

"There are rules about building fences, you know. Property lines. Setbacks. All kinds of fun stuff."

"I'm not talking about a stockade fence," she told him as she stepped free from the tangle of Oscar's leash. "He's a tiny dog. It doesn't take much to keep him inside."

"Legalities don't care if it's six inches or six feet." He shrugged. "A fence is a fence."

Her neighbor was as annoying as he was attractive. "Obviously I'd look into the legalities before having one installed. And that's an interesting mug for a guy who claims he doesn't own the cat who lives in his house."

He looked at the cat print as if he hadn't noticed it before. "It's not my cat. And it's not my mug, either."

She waited, but he didn't add to the statement. He was a puzzle and the urge to try to figure him out was strong, but she had neither the time nor the patience to wheedle more pieces out of him.

Oscar started walking toward the house and, when he reached the end of his leash, gave her a questioning look. Though she had a pickup baggie in the pocket of her cardigan, she hadn't been paying attention and she had no desire to go on a poop hunt in her pajamas with Cam watching her. She'd come back later when he wasn't outside. Since he was staying for the summer and had mentioned spreadsheets, he was probably working remotely and would spend his days inside with his computer.

"I'll leave you to somebody else's mug, then," she said and he lifted it in a brief salute before she followed Oscar up the steps to the deck and into the house.

Sophie was awake, curled up on the sofa in a light throw blanket. "It's freezing here."

"My little California baby." She smiled at her daughter and then gave Oscar a treat because Devin had spoiled him rotten and rewarding him with fake bacon had been the only way to house-train him. "You'll get used to it."

They both would, she thought. While she might be from New Hampshire, she'd gone to California for college and stayed there. It had been a long time since she'd experienced a New England winter, and based on one June morning, she had some toughening up to do herself.

"Mommy, when is my stuff coming?"

"In a couple more days, sweetie. I didn't know exactly how long the drive would take us and I didn't want the truck to get here first."

They'd each packed what they couldn't live without, filling the back of the SUV with clothes, books, a few toys and the small box of Devin's things she couldn't part with or risk losing in the move. The rest, the moving company would bring. Thankfully she'd considered the downsizing in space and had done a rather brutal decluttering before the move so she and Sophie wouldn't be too overwhelmed by boxes.

"What are we going to do today?"

Meredith considered the question as she put the last of the pastries she'd bought on the road on the table. Some orange juice bought at a convenience store before they got to town rounded out breakfast. She'd packed food and treats for Oscar and nonperishable snacks for her and Sophie, but day-old baked goods were getting old.

"We need to buy some food," she said, setting her notebook on the table in front of her.

She used to have a huge fancy planner with every day broken down to the hour, but the hectic schedule that came with being Devin Price's wife had died with him. As friends and social commitments had fallen away and Sophie had less and less interest in interaction with her classmates, the mostly empty planner pages had served as a depressing daily reminder of the loss in her life, so she'd tossed it.

Now she had a small hardcover notebook that was always close at hand or in her purse and she noted down things she needed to do and information she might want to reference again.

Using the tattered ribbon bookmark to open it to the current page, she added *install a fence* and then, after remembering her conversation—such as it was—with Cam, she added *ask town hall about fence rules*.

"I only have sixteen pages left in my book," Sophie said in much the same tone as a person would announce an impending apocalypse.

"We'd better go to the library, then." She added that to the list, along with grocery shopping. Sometimes she added obvious things just for the pleasure of crossing them off. "We'll get library cards and some books, and maybe some movies, too, if they have any good ones."

"Do you think they have a summer reading program?"

Meredith smiled at the question. While she knew her daughter just liked having fun charts to fill in with the many books she read, she hoped they had a program as much as Sophie did. It would be a perfect way for her to meet kids with similar interests.

"I don't know, but they probably do."

"You could ask Cam!" Sophie seemed delighted by her solution to her mother's lack of a definitive answer.

"Mr. Maguire," she corrected gently. "And I doubt he would know, honey. I haven't seen any children next door and I don't know if he has any."

Sophie didn't ask if she'd seen any other children in the immediate area. There was a large wooded area between their house and the neighbor on the other side, and most of the homes on their side of the bay seemed to be summer cottages—all as or more expensive-looking than hers, except for Cam's—so she wasn't sure any of them would be occupied during the week. If they were lucky, though, there might be a few families with young kids who'd spend more than weekends on the lake.

While Sophie had always been happy to amuse herself, she'd taken it to a new level after her dad passed away. Or maybe it was just Meredith's percep-tion of her daughter. Instead of seeming a little shy, she was withdrawn. Instead of enjoying her books, she seemed to be hiding in them. But when it became obvious Sophie had no interest in friendships any-more and preferred to be alone, Meredith and their family therapist had discussed how she and Sophie might both benefit from a clean break from the life that felt empty without Devin in it.

"When are Grandma and Grandpa coming?" Sophie asked, dragging Meredith away from her thoughts.

"Tomorrow." Her parents had moved out of Black-berry Bay shortly after Meredith left for college, choosing to move into a condo in Concord for the second phase of their lives. It was only an hour away, and she considered that the perfect distance. Close enough so they could be an active part of Sophie's life, but far enough away so she and her mother wouldn't trip over each other and visits would be planned in advance. "Are you excited to see them?"

"Yes, even though it's hard to remember them a little."

The last time Meredith had visited her parents, Sophie had been too young to remember it. Her par-ents had flown to San Diego for Devin's funeral and then almost a year ago, but even with the occasional FaceTime chat, it wasn't easy for Sophie to bond with her grandparents. And since Devin's mother had died before Meredith had met him and his father wasn't a very warm or personable man, she wanted Sophie to have her maternal grandparents in her life on a more regular basis. It would be good for her.

After they ate breakfast, Sophie headed to her bedroom to get dressed with Oscar in her arms. Meredith had once told her she shouldn't carry him everywhere or he'd get even more spoiled than he already was, but Sophie had argued that he was tiny and by carrying him, he was close enough she could tell him stories and secrets. She hadn't had the heart to tell her to put Oscar down after that, and now she carried him everywhere.

Meredith got dressed and then went into the backyard to clean up after Oscar. It took her a few minutes to find the spot, and she'd just tied off the bag when she realized her neighbor hadn't gone inside to work.

He was stretched out in a hammock by the water, his weight stretching the netting and making it conform to the curve of his body. Those feelings she hadn't felt in a long time stirred inside her again, and heat climbed into her face.

Turning abruptly, she walked up the steps and hesitated a moment before setting the bag on the edge of the railing to deal with after she'd bought a small garbage can for under the deck.

We definitely need a fence, she thought, resisting

the urge to glance back at the hammock. Preferably a very tall one she couldn't see through.

Cam did a damn good job of pretending he didn't notice the sexy mom next door was outside again, if he did say so himself.

He'd been tempted to tease her a little about her task, but she'd already shown him they weren't on the same page when it came to humor and he didn't want to make it any worse. Verbally sparring with his neighbor had been amusing to him until he realized she hadn't caught that he was joking. The last thing he wanted to do was upset a woman who'd obviously been through enough in the last couple of years.

Turning his head, he looked out over the bay, trying to take in the tranquility of the view. He needed tranquility in his life. A lot of it, preferably. In the two weeks he'd been in Blackberry Bay, he'd already noticed the tension headaches that had been plaguing him for several years had abated and he slept better.

It was remarkable considering the circumstances that had brought him here. The letter had been on his desk with the rest of his mail and he could remember hesitating before slicing the envelope open, though he couldn't say why.

A lawyer telling him his biological grandmother had passed away shouldn't have affected him. He'd never met her. He wasn't even supposed to know he had a "biological" side of the family. The miserably unhappy Maguire family never openly spoke about the time his mother had left his father and fallen for some random guy. They certainly never talked about how she'd discovered she was pregnant right around the same time she discovered she really missed her husband's bank account, but Cam had pieced together the story on his own over the years.

Calvin III had needed a son to get his own father off his back and Melissa needed financial security. The random guy was given a check, papers were signed and nobody ever explained why Cam didn't share the look of all the Maguire men, without looking like his mother, either. But he knew. People whispered. Veiled barbs flung at a spouse during an argument weren't always very veiled. And his paternal grandmother had never forgiven her daughter-in-law, and Cam had overheard a heated argument about a check before he was really old enough to know what a check even was.

The secrets of his birth had never been a secret, but he'd never summoned the courage to ask the identity of his biological father. It had never seemed worth the fallout within the family, since apparently the man had walked away in exchange for money.

And so every time he looked in the mirror, Cam was reminded his presence in the Maguire family was tolerated because a fourth generation on the let-terhead brought the illusion of stability to a business.

Then he got the letter. He hadn't known about Carolina Archambault, but she'd known about him. And she'd left him her cottage at the lake because, according to the handwritten letter delivered with the legal notice, he was the only family she had left. Her son—Cam's biological father—had died before her. The lawyer asked Cam to visit Blackberry Bay as soon as possible to assume management of the estate, which consisted of the cottage and his grandmother's cat, which was waiting for him at the local shelter.

He had the staff and the money to make it all go away without any more effort on his part than delegating the tasks. But the lawyer had included her obituary and the photo had punched him in the gut. Even though the image was black-and-white, he could tell he had her eyes. And unlike his own, which probably gave away nothing but emotionless deter-mination to care about his father's business enough to keep showing up, hers shone with warmth and humor. The woman in the photograph would have loved him with her whole heart, he thought.

Cam lied to his parents about joining a prospec-tive wife at her family's summer home and, after assuring them he could work remotely, packed the necessities into his car and drove to Blackberry Bay.

Air left his body with a hard whoosh when a mass

of black fur landed solidly on his stomach with no warning. Elinor knit his shirt and underlying skin for a few seconds—and he suffered the light claw pricks because he'd learned the hard way reacting made it so much more painful—before she settled on his chest, staring at him.

"Hi, cat." She blinked. "Okay, I'm not very good at this. I've never had a pet, but I'm trying my best. So maybe you could do me a favor and not pick on the little dog next door, okay?"

She seemed disinterested and he chuckled, which was rewarded with her claws pricking at his skin again for a few seconds. He never would have imagined himself talking to an animal, never having had one around, but they were surprisingly good listeners. Sure, he had a feeling Elinor could be a little judgmental, but at least she couldn't verbalize it.

"Mr. Maguire?"

The little voice was close and it startled Cam. His jerky movement, as small as it was, startled Elinor, and it took everything he had not to curse in front of the little girl as the cat launched herself off his chest.

"Hi, Sophie," he said once the chaos subsided and he was on his feet.

"Can I ask you a question?" She was standing right around where the property line was and her anxiety was clear on her face.

"Of course you can."

"Can you tell me where you bought that?" She nodded toward the hammock. "I want to ask my mom to buy me one, but I don't know where they come from."

"Unfortunately, it was here when I got here, so I don't know." He frowned at the hammock on the stand, with the sunshade attached over it. "I don't think my grandmother was much of an online shopper, so it probably came from a local store."

"Okay, thank you." She started to walk away.

"Hey, Sophie. If you tell your mom you want one, I'm sure she'll be able to find one. And they probably make smaller ones, too, so it would be easier to get in and out of."

"I need a big one because it's for me and Oscar and my books."

"Ah. That makes sense. I'll tell you what. If I'm not using my hammock, you and Oscar and your books can use it if it's okay with your mom and she shows you how to get in and out of it without hurting yourself."

Once she'd gone back in the house, he took a few minutes to adjust the metal stand, lowering the hammock as close to the ground as it would go. He might have to adjust it again when he used it so his butt didn't rest on the ground, but he'd leave it this way when he wasn't using it so Sophie wouldn't get hurt.

Twenty minutes later, just as he was opening his

laptop to get some work done, there was a knock on the door and he saw Meredith on the other side of the screen slider. His pulse quickened for a few seconds and he tried to tell himself it was just annoyance at being interrupted again. With a sigh, he closed the computer and walked over to open it.

"Good morning, neighbor," he said, leaning against the jamb.

"Good morning. Sophie told me you offered her the use of your hammock and I just wanted to make sure it was really okay with you and not a misunderstanding."

"It's okay with me, but did she also tell you the part where you have to teach her how to get in and out of the thing without hurting herself or the dog?"

She smiled and brushed her hair away from her face. "She did. I'll make sure she knows how to use it. And thank you. She loves to curl up with Oscar and read, and a hammock is more fun than a deck chair. I'm going to buy her one of her own as soon as I find one."

"You should get matching ones so you have one for yourself. They're surprisingly relaxing. You do know how to get in a hammock, right?"

She put her hand on her hip and arched a brow at him, which made him chuckle. "You forget, I'm the one from here. Of course I've used a hammock."

"As an adult?" He laughed when she looked away,

clearly not wanting to answer. He wasn't much of a hammock expert since he'd owned one for only a couple of weeks—and thank goodness he hadn't had an audience for his first few tries—but he suspected they were less intimidating to children.

"I'll let you get back to what you were doing," she said, taking a step back.

For some reason, he didn't really want her to leave. "I wasn't doing anything important."

"I have to take Sophie into town. My parents are coming to visit tomorrow and I have so many errands to run today. And we desperately need food. But thanks again for the use of your hammock. Maybe I'll show her how to use it later today, if you're sure you don't mind."

"I'm sure." As a matter of fact, he was looking forward to watching this woman practice her rusty hammock skills in his backyard. Maybe he'd even pour himself a drink and sit on his deck.

It wasn't until Meredith was gone and he'd turned back to the chaotic clutter Carolina had surrounded herself with that the realization Meredith had grown up in Blackberry Bay really sunk in. And her parents were visiting tomorrow.

They might have all known his grandmother. Her parents might even have known his biological father. Feeling a bit shaky all of a sudden, he sat on the edge of the floral love seat and stared at his closed laptop.

Maybe watching his sexy neighbor wrestle with the hammock wouldn't be the only benefit of her moving in next door.

Chapter Three

Blackberry Bay had hardly changed at all since Meredith left for college in California, and yet it felt as strange to her as a location she'd never visited.

She wasn't sure if it was because she was walking down the street holding her little girl's hand or maybe it was the life experiences she'd had since leaving. The last time this town had been her actual home, she'd been eighteen and looking forward to college. She couldn't have known then that she'd meet Devin, have a daughter and build a joyful life on the other side of the country. Or that it would all come crashing down thanks to a second of thoughtlessness by one reckless driver.

phie beamed as she was handed her first library card from her new town. And she talked Meredith into buying one of the Spurr Memorial Library canvas tote bags they were selling as a fund-raiser to carry their books home in.

But the highlight of Sophie's day was definitely signing up for the summer reading program, and it made Meredith happy, as well. While Sophie was in it for the charts and stickers, Meredith saw enough fun social events on the calendar to ensure her daughter would already know quite a few of the kids in town before school started.

"Let's put the books in the car, and then we can buy some groceries," she said when they finally left the library. They'd spent more time there than Meredith had anticipated, but she shouldn't have been surprised. There was little Sophie liked more than libraries and bookstores.

"I'm tired," Sophie said, with a hint of a whine creeping into her voice.

"We did the fun errand first because it's too hot to leave groceries in the car, but we have to do the not-fun errand, too."

"I want to read one of my new books in the hammock with Oscar."

Meredith hit the button to unlock her SUV's doors and set the tote bag on the back seat, where Sophie would be able to reach it during the ride home. But then she very firmly closed the door and locked it again.

"We'll see if we have time for the hammock later, Sophie. But we're out of food and we can't put off grocery shopping." She gave her daughter a pointed look. "And if you're too tired for shopping, then you're too tired to learn how to get in the hammock."

Sophie sighed and stuck her bottom lip out a bit, but she didn't argue as Meredith took her hand and led her toward the market. In the future she'd probably make a master list and make the trip into the city, with its big-box stores, for nonperishables once a month, but she didn't have the time or the energy right now.

They managed to make it through the entire list without Sophie having a meltdown, but Meredith wasn't surprised when she fell asleep within minutes of the car starting. It wasn't a very long drive back to the house, but she knew her daughter needed the nap, so she surrendered to driving around Blackberry Bay, refamiliarizing herself with the streets and enjoying the memories that surfaced as she explored.

The historic look and feel of the town had hardly changed at all, which wasn't surprising since the historical society and planning board worked hard to preserve the history of the town. They didn't even allow vinyl siding within a certain radius of the downtown district, so the buildings were all brick, cedar shakes or clapboards diligently painted in town-approved colors. The larger chain stores that had grown to be a necessary part of almost every town's economy were all on the outskirts, out of view of the tourists.

Most of the stores along the waterfront stretch of Main Street catered to the tourists, with everything from boutiques offering overpriced swimwear to scuba equipment. Ice-cream shops and gourmet coffee bars. There were shops offering skiing equipment along with gear for other winter endeavors, since they were close to the ski area.

On Cedar Street, she passed the café, which she remembered as having great food, and a new bookstore with a fun summer window display. There was a consignment shop, and she saw that a hair salon had gone in where the television-repair shop used to be.

The original Blackberry Bay schoolhouse had been turned into the historical society's headquarters, and there were larger schools on the outskirts of town, including the three-story brick high school she'd graduated from. If Sophie hadn't been sleeping, she would have shown her the elementary school she'd be attending, with the brightly colored garden mural painted on the brick front wall.

She wondered, as she turned around in the school parking lot, how many of the people she'd graduated with still lived in Blackberry Bay. It was a beautiful town, but its primary industry was tourism, and a lot of the kids who went off to college didn't move back. But some of them still had to be around, and she was looking forward to renewing some old acquaintances.

Twenty minutes would be enough to recharge Sophie's batteries without throwing off her sleep schedule, so Meredith finally drove home and pulled into the driveway.

Her new neighbor's sleek, dark sedan—which she knew from her California social circle was *not* cheap—was parked in his driveway, but she tried to ignore it as she killed her engine and got out.

She couldn't help wondering what he did, though, that enabled him to work remotely, if that was actually what he meant when he said he'd be reading over spreadsheets. It didn't seem like the kind of thing a person did for fun, so she assumed it had to do with his job. She knew several of the people who worked for Devin had done so from home, traveling to the offices only for important meetings.

When she got out of her car, leaving the door open so it didn't get warm for Sophie, she was surprised to see Cam walk around from her backyard with the cat in his arms.

He paused when he saw her, and then met her near her front door. "Hi again. Sorry to trespass, but I was looking for Elinor. Again."

"I hope Oscar didn't bark the whole time we were gone," she said, since her dog was currently barking rather enthusiastically.

"Like you said, it's more of a high-pitched yip." Before she could apologize, he grinned. "And only when I used a tree branch to scratch at the windows."

She laughed, telling herself he *had* to be joking. She hoped. And considering the mischievous gleam in his eyes, he'd probably been joking about the muzzle, too.

"Actually he's barking because Queen Elinor here was pacing back and forth in front of your slider, taunting him. That's why I came to get her."

The cat looked unimpressed by the accusation, and lifted her chin when Meredith reached out to give her a little scratch. "You're a little troublemaker, huh?"

"A massive troublemaker is more like it. I didn't know cats grew this big, to be honest. Where's Sophie?"

"She fell asleep in the car, which was a blessing. That child definitely needed a nap."

"All this fresh lake air," he said with a chuckle. "Do you want me to carry her into the house for you?"

Meredith felt sucker punched by an image of this man carrying her sleeping daughter, and she hoped it didn't show on her face. Devin had often carried

Sophie up to bed when she was little, and then he'd tuck her in and kiss her forehead. Those were the little moments she missed the most, and it hurt to imagine another man filling that role.

Someday, she thought. She *wanted* Sophie to have a father figure, and Meredith certainly didn't want to live the rest of her life alone, but she hadn't thought about what that future might look like yet.

"Meredith?"

"Oh." She shook her head and focused her attention back on the *now*. "Thank you for the offer, but I'm going to wake her up. If she sleeps too long, I'll never get her to bed tonight. She's reached that fun age where she's outgrown regular naps, but still needs one now and then."

He nodded, his expression making it clear he had no idea what she was talking about. "Okay. Well, I should get this monster in the house and get some work done. Hopefully your dog will settle down now that she's not flipping her tail at him through the glass."

Once she'd gotten a groggy Sophie into the house and taken Oscar into the backyard—where he was a lot more focused on the scent of Elinor than doing his business—she made multiple trips to carry all the groceries in.

There were a lot fewer cabinets than their old house had, but Meredith turned putting the groceries away into a game. Sophie, who was in a good mood after her nap, enjoyed sorting the cans, even though she liked them arranged by color, with no regard to what was actually in each can.

Meredith went through the motions, but her mind kept straying back to the idea of having a man around again. Not Cam, of course, because he wasn't her type and he was only around for the summer, but somebody. She poked at the idea, as if she was probing a sore tooth with the tip of her tongue to see if it still hurt.

And it did. But it was more like a chronic ache than acute pain, and she wasn't sure what to make of that. Maybe a fresh start would do her as much good as it hopefully would her daughter.

I've been summoned by the town selectmen again. They think if they complain about my cottage enough and with big legal-sounding words, I'll do what they want. You'd think people smart enough to use words like heretofore *in a sentence would know better than that.*

People should pay less attention to how something looks and care more how it makes a person feel. This cottage makes me happy. I don't have a lot. I lost my Thomas so many years ago, and then our Michael. I never got to hold my grandchild. It's just me and Elinor, but we're happy and this cottage is part of the reason why.

Who cares if a home is painted pink instead of cream and the trim is turquoise instead of Colonial blue or whatever the town ordinance says it can be? It's my home and if they don't like it, they should stop driving by and slowing down to take pictures to send me with sternly worded letters.

On the plus side, I have some lovely photos of my beautiful little cottage on the lake.

Always look on the plus side. You'll sleep better at night.

Cam closed the journal and leaned his head back against the couch cushion with a sigh.

Carolina Archambault—the grandmother he'd never known—had been quite a woman. The journals she'd bequeathed to him weren't exactly of the "dear diary" kind. The entries read more like letters to somebody. Maybe just to the world at large. Or maybe to him. His gut told him they had the feel of a woman sharing her life with the grandson she knew was out there somewhere.

He was supposed to be reviewing the many possible ways pending tax legislation could impact the company's bottom line—or more accurately, reviewing the reports Accounting and Legal had generated, and then summarizing all the info into a few bullet points and a recommendation for his father. And he'd intended to do just that. He'd even opened his laptop before reaching for the journal he'd left next to it.

He blamed the cottage in general. It wasn't really the kind of place for corporate goings-on. But more specifically, it was the framed photo that hung across the room in his line of vision that kept distracting him.

Michael Archambault.

His biological father. Cam had already lost count of the number of times he'd looked at the picture, which had been the first thing that caught his eye the day he arrived.

Cam looked like him. He had the man's hair and eyes and mouth, and he could even see the similarities in their expression based on photos he'd seen of himself. The photo definitely answered the question "Why can't you be more like your father?" which he'd heard countless times from his grandfather Calvin Anthony II before he'd passed away.

Because Calvin Anthony Maguire III wasn't his father. This man was, and Cam had been robbed of the opportunity to ever know him.

Fur brushing his hand was the only warning he got before Elinor leaped to the back of the couch. Thanks to her size, the space she chose to curl up on included the top of his head, and he let her be.

When had he become a guy who could spend a summer in a small, cluttered cottage and wear a cat like a hat?

Trying to imagine his parents' expressions if they could see him right now made him chuckle. Or his mother's, anyway. Stone was his father's only expression. Though his mother would definitely not be amused.

Considering how angry they were right now, he wouldn't be surprised. It was a quiet, simmering anger, of course. No yelling or swearing involved. But he knew his father well enough to read the displeasure between the lines of terse emails. Working remotely was feasible, of course—one could read reports and handle spreadsheets from anywhere— but his father didn't like the appearance of him being away. The empty seat at the conference table was obviously getting under dear old Dad's skin.

Right now, in this moment, he didn't care. With Elinor purring on top of his head and the faint sound of laughter from the little girl next door soothing his nerves, he was strangely content to relax in the strange new world.

It was an adjustment, for sure. His first few nights in town, he'd stayed at the inn, and even in what passed for a downtown district in Blackberry Bay, the silence had been unnerving. He'd had to leave the television on in order to sleep.

There had been a lot of adjustments in the first few days. Not only could he not have food delivered at ten o'clock at night if he got lost in work and forgot to eat, but he couldn't have food delivered at noon. No delivery. No Uber Eats. No Uber at all.

And then there was the cottage. Shabby inside, with very few modern touches. He'd had to order an overnight delivery of a Keurig and coffee pods. And there was barely room for his few belongings because Carolina had apparently never passed up a rummage sale. He'd try to focus on the bones of the cottage and it *was* solidly built, but everything inside it should have been replaced around the time he was born. And who installed a cat door next to a sliding glass door? The cottage was a chaos his orderly brain had trouble comprehending.

There was also the fact people were a little more friendly, which was good. But they also weren't shy about asking a lot of questions, which wasn't as good. As far as he was aware, Carolina's lawyer was the only person who knew the entire truth of his arrival in town. And Meredith, he supposed, though she didn't know all the details. But he'd been to the market, a gas station and the hardware store, and at each stop, he'd been asked about staying in Carolina's cottage. He'd dodged the questions the best he could, making it sound as though he was just a summer renter, but he knew this wasn't the kind of place a secret would stay a secret very long. And since he'd made the decision to stay in Blackberry Bay and learn about the Archambault family rather than having somebody sell it off for him, he was eventually going to have to reach out to people who'd known Michael and Carolina.

But for now, he was content to sit and relax. Truly relax, which went beyond just closing his laptop for the night. There was no tension at all in his body, and he felt as if he could happily sit there indefinitely without feeling the urge to get up and do something productive.

Then the dog next door barked and it must have displeased Elinor, who reacted by extending her claws. She didn't grip, but the very tips pricked at his skin and he wanted to pick her up, but he was afraid that if he tried to move her, she'd really grab hold of his scalp.

Luckily, with her nap disturbed anyway, she decided to move on. As she made her way to the floor without drawing any of his blood, he gave her a stern look. "I think we're going to need to establish some boundaries if we're going to make it through the summer."

She just twitched her tail and walked away, leaving him to wonder what was going to happen if they *did* make it through the summer together. There was no way he could bring her back to the city with him.

Even if he wanted an enormous black cat shedding all over everything he owned, which he didn't, Elinor liked her freedom. He couldn't imagine her being happy as an inside-only cat for the rest of her life, and that was what she would have to be.

But he couldn't just leave her at the shelter again. Elinor was proud and more than a little spoiled, and she couldn't have been happy there. She'd even gone out of her way to show him gratitude when he brought her back to her home, in the form of head-butting him over and over for a solid hour. He assumed it was gratitude, at least. She might have been trying to shove him out the door, for all he knew about cats.

When he caught himself considering whether or not he could rent the cottage out with the stipulation the tenant had to love and care for Elinor for the remainder of her days, Cam decided it was time to get off the couch and do something.

The cardboard boxes he'd bought were still propped, flat and empty, against a wall, waiting to be filled. It was his intention to fill them with items that were obviously personal, and then bring in people to sort and pack the rest for sale or donation. But Carolina had accumulated so much *stuff*, he didn't even know where to begin. And every time he picked up a trinket or photo, he'd wonder about it and find himself going back to her journals.

He was going to need more than one summer at the rate he was going, but he still didn't grab the packing tape and build a box to fill. Instead, he grabbed a bottle of lemonade and went out onto the back deck to get some fresh air.

His neighbors were sitting on the double swing on their dock, their heads together as they talked and laughed. But it was only a minute before Sophie looked up and spotted him.

"Mr. Maguire!" She jumped up, causing her mother to reach out for her shirt in case she went right off the dock, and then she ran toward him. The little dog ran with her, and Cam held his breath, hoping they wouldn't get tangled together and fall.

For a second, he felt a pang of irritation. It was definitely going to be a long summer if he couldn't even enjoy a drink on his own deck without a kid running over. But he couldn't hold on to it. The little girl was adorable and a welcome interruption from his brooding.

"Why is your cat named Elinor, Mr. Maguire?"

He winced at the formal name because it reminded him of who he was and what he was *supposed* to be doing right now, which was keeping his eye on the company's bottom line at all times. "I'm not sure, actually. My grandmother named her."

"Oh." Sophie sighed and her disappointment was

almost palpable. "It's a funny name for a cat and my mom said you might know."

"Sorry, kiddo. But if I find out why, I'll definitely tell you."

"Oscar, no!"

The shout from Meredith made Cam realize he'd left his slider open when he stepped outside, and her little dog had taken that as invitation. He also didn't seem to care that Meredith was telling him no.

"He can't hurt anything," he reassured Meredith when she reached the deck, flushed and a little out of breath.

"He can't just go in people's houses like that."

"Mr. Maguire left the door open," Sophie argued, and he appreciated the way she came to her dog's defense.

"Should I go get him, or…"

When Meredith let the words trail away, he realized she was asking him if she should go in or not, and he wasn't sure what to say. He didn't really want them inside because he didn't want to answer a ton of questions about all of Carolina's things. But there was a good chance the dog wasn't going to let a strange man pick him up.

Before he could say anything, there was a single high-pitched yip and the small white ball of fluff streaked out the door and past them with Elinor hot on his heels. Oscar went straight down the stairs and back to his own yard without stopping, and Sophie ran after him.

Elinor, however, stopped on the deck and rubbed against Cam's leg a few times. Then, intruder driven off, she jumped onto the patio table and stretched out in the sun.

"Sorry about that," Meredith said, her mouth curving into a smile. "But I doubt he's going to go in your house again anytime soon."

"I hope she didn't hurt him," Cam said. "She's kind of a beast, and her claws are no joke."

"Sophie's cuddling him now. She would be yelling if he had any blood on him, so I think Elinor just scared him. And let him know who's boss in this neighborhood."

He was relieved, and also very conscious they were now alone on the deck. He could see Sophie and Oscar, but he was pretty sure she couldn't hear them from where they were sitting in the grass. "I've been wanting to ask you something, but not in front of Sophie."

"Okay." Anxiety tightened her lips, and he realized she was bracing for a personal question.

"I was hoping maybe she could call me Cam."

"Oh. I…" She frowned and looked across the yard at her daughter. "It's usually a hard-and-fast rule, but since you asked, it would be rude to force the issue, I guess."

He was going to have to give her some kind of an explanation, though he didn't want to get too deeply into the why of things. "I'm working through some family issues right now, and hearing *Mr. Maguire* makes me think of my dad. We're not in a great place and it kills my mood a bit."

"I'm sorry. That must be hard." She looked at him for a long moment, as though she wanted to ask questions about the situation, but then her face softened and she smiled. "And yes, I suppose Sophie can call you Cam, since you prefer it. And we're neighbors, after all."

"Do you want a lemonade or something?" he asked, because he'd had company manners drilled into him since he was practically an infant.

"No, thank you. It looks like it's going to rain soon, so I need to have Sophie put away any books or dog toys she took out and then get them inside."

"Maybe another time," he said, and even as the words left his mouth, he had no idea where they came from. He wasn't here to make friends, no matter how pretty they were. He had work to do and a cottage to declutter and prepare for market.

And the look she gave him made it clear she was as surprised by the comment as he was. She frowned a little before giving him a friendly but distant smile. "Maybe. I apologize again for Oscar's intrusion. And for Sophie's, I guess. I'll talk to her about respecting boundaries, but it's harder without a fence, I think."

He laughed. "You seem very determined to put up a fence between us."

The smile faded. "Fences help everybody remember where they're supposed to be. And you know what they say. Good fences make good neighbors."

Cam wasn't sure if that message was as directed at him as she'd made it sound, but he'd do well to take it to heart. As she crossed the invisible boundary into her own yard, he turned around and went back inside, leaving Elinor to enjoy the last few minutes of sun before the rain hit.

Chapter Four

Meredith couldn't remember the last time she'd laughed so hard. Her stomach hurt almost as much as her butt, though neither was as injured as her dignity.

"Maybe you should sit in the swing on our dock," Sophie said before dissolving into giggles again as Meredith glared at the hammock.

"I can do this."

"I'm starting to wonder if the property insurance on this cottage covers neighbors falling out of my hammock."

The deep male voice behind her made Meredith whirl around, her cheeks hot, and she almost stumbled. Cam put out his hand to steady her, and the touch on her bare arm did nothing to cool the heat in her face.

"I guess it's been longer than I thought," she admitted reluctantly. "I also didn't think you were home."

"I wasn't. And your fierce guard dog was too busy laughing at you to notice me, I guess."

"Elinor's been sitting on the deck railing, watching. I'm pretty sure she laughed, too."

"Do you need some help?"

She wasn't sure how exactly he could help her, and she definitely couldn't see any way he could help her into the hammock without touching her. The thought made her cheeks burn, so she turned away.

"Thanks, but I think it's time to quit for the day. My parents will be here soon and here I am with dirt under my nails and grass stains on my butt."

Then she cursed herself for saying that as she had to bend over to pick up the sandals she'd kicked off into the grass.

"I tried to show her," Sophie said, hopping into the hammock as if she'd been doing it her entire life. "But she's not very good at it."

Oscar stood up so his front paws were on the edge of the hammock, and Sophie managed to hook him by whatever a dog's armpits were called and haul him in without tipping them onto the ground.

"You are, though," he said. "I'm impressed."

"Showoff," Meredith muttered, and Sophie giggled. "Now that Mr.…Cam is home, we should give him his yard back, though."

"I don't mind," he said quickly, and she got the impression he really meant it.

"See, Mom? Cam doesn't mind. I told you."

"That's very nice of him, but your grandparents will be here soon. We should clean up a little."

"They don't care if I'm dirty," Sophie shot back, folding her arms across her chest, and Meredith watched Cam press his lips together to keep from smiling because he was obviously smart enough to see a battle of wills was about to begin and he wanted no part of it.

"Sophie Grace Price, do not make me tell you again."

She didn't have to break out the dreaded middle name often, but when she did, it usually worked. Sophie sighed very dramatically and—after tucking Oscar against her chest—rolled out of the hammock. She landed neatly on her feet and set the dog in the grass.

She definitely hadn't gotten her hammock skills from her mother.

"Grandma!" Sophie's sudden exuberant shout seemed to echo across the bay, and Meredith turned to see her parents walking across her lawn. They must have heard them in the backyard and walked around the house.

Oscar, of course, barked and ran in circles as first Sophie and then Meredith hugged them. Her mother gave her an extra squeeze, of course, because they talked on the phone regularly, but it had been a while since they'd seen each other.

"You found yourself a beautiful spot," her dad said, taking in the view. "I always did love this side of the bay, since it's quiet."

"It used to be quiet, anyway," Meredith said before trying to shush a very excited Oscar. When Sophie got excited, so did the dog, even if he wasn't sure what was happening.

Her mom gave her a questioning look and then tilted her head in Cam's direction. Meredith realized she'd have to introduce him, since they were all currently standing in his yard.

"Mom and Dad, this is our neighbor, Cam Maguire. Cam, these are my parents—Neal and Erin Lane." She watched them shake hands, and then, before she could herd her family back onto her own property, her dad and Cam were deep in conversation about the lake and fishing.

Or rather, her father was talking about the lake and fishing. Cam was mostly nodding along and throwing in the occasional comment, which made her wonder if he actually knew anything about the topic at hand.

"He seems nice," her mom said in a voice barely above a whisper.

"You got all that from 'nice to meet you, Mrs. Lane,' did you?" Meredith rolled her eyes, but since they were both looking at the men, who'd made their way to the water's edge with Sophie, her mother didn't see it.

"Don't get like that," Erin said. "All I'm saying is that your neighbor seems nice. I'm your mother. I don't want you living next door to a grumpy ax murderer or anything."

"I haven't seen an ax yet."

"Good. I want you to be happy here. When I got out of the car and heard you and Sophie laughing, I swear that was the first time since the accident that I've drawn a full breath. I've been so worried about both of you."

"Don't even *start* thinking it has anything to do with Cam," she warned.

"I don't care what makes you happy as long as you both keep laughing like that."

Thankfully, her mom let the subject drop and was content to watch Sophie walking with her grandfather, her little hand tucked into his. It was a small thing, but to Meredith it was one more sign she'd made the right decision in coming back to Blackberry Bay.

"This is a perfect yard for a cookout, Meredith," her dad said as the men joined them again.

"True, but this is actually Cam's yard, and buying a barbecue grill is still on my list of things to do."

Way down on the list, too, since they'd never done a lot of grilling in California. She'd been thinking about buying one of those small indoor grilling machines, but her dad was right. Their backyard was perfect for a cookout.

"I have a grill," Cam said, nodding toward the far end of his deck. "I'd be happy to host a cookout if you have something to grill. And some side dishes. I have a bag of chips, I think."

"Mommy bought steaks at the market," Sophie volunteered.

"Perfect," Erin said over Sophie's excited squeal. There was no way for Meredith to politely decline the offer at this point, so she gave her mother a stern look. She got an innocent smile in return, which she hoped was genuine.

She wanted no part of her neighbor getting caught up in some kind of maternal matchmaking scheme. He was being polite. Neighborly. That was all it was and all it was ever going to be.

But on the plus side, she didn't have to cook and there would be very little cleanup, which definitely made her happy. Freedom from that domestic chore was ringing through her head when she looked at Cam, and it wasn't until he raised an eyebrow that she realized he could see that joy.

Then his face softened and he gave her a smile that weakened her knees. She decided he didn't need to know she'd been giving thanks for paper plates. He could think whatever he wanted if he kept smiling at her that way.

This is all Carolina's fault.

Living in her cottage, surrounded by the clutter of a long, full life, was rubbing off on him somehow. It was the only explanation he could come up with for offering to host a backyard cookout for people he didn't even know.

Okay, maybe not the *only* reason. The smile he'd put on Meredith's face probably had something to do with it, too. She and her daughter both seemed to have *resting serious face*, which probably wasn't even a real thing, but it applied to them. Even though he was in well over his head, as far as this cookout went, Meredith's smile and Sophie's squeal of delight were worth it.

All he had to do was cook some meat over a gas-fired flame.

He stared at the gas grill, doing his best to believe his own pep talk. He could do this. Sure, he was born and raised in Manhattan and had never actually grilled food before. But how hard could it be?

After pulling up videos online, he'd had to sneak a few photos of the identifying information on the grill so he could go back inside and find model-specific tutorials. Apparently there were a lot of different kinds of gas grills. But he'd finally found some instructions that seemed applicable and, fingers crossed, he wouldn't blow his eyebrows off.

It would be a lot simpler to hand the process over to Neal and let him handle it. But there was something about passing the spatula over to another man while Meredith was watching that had him reluctant to admit he hadn't mastered this skill. It was stupid, he knew. But he wanted to grill these people some steaks.

Meredith stepping up close to him only reinforced his determination to get it done. He was *not* going to embarrass himself in front of her.

"Have you ever used a grill before?" she asked in a voice that was barely above a whisper.

"What kind of question is that?"

"You told me you're from New York City."

"Believe it or not, they have barbecue grills in the city."

"But have you personally manned one?"

He was so distracted by how close she was to him that he could barely think. She was trying to keep her parents from overhearing their conversation, which he knew on a logical level, but the closer her head got to his—he could smell her hair and it smelled delicious—the more logic flew out the window.

"I've been standing very nearby when it was done," he admitted.

"We could start small. Maybe some hot dogs."

He did his best to look offended, but he didn't exactly have the high ground. And it wasn't a bad idea. "We'll leave hot dogs as the emergency backup."

She chuckled. "How many YouTube videos did you watch?"

"As many as I could find."

"Good. I like my steaks a perfect medium, by the way."

He laughed, and pointed the spatula at her. "You're pretty picky for a woman with grass stains on her butt."

When she laughed with him, he experienced a strange moment of awareness that made his chest ache. Standing over a grill in the backyard, laughing with a beautiful woman while a dog chased a little girl around the yard to the amusement of her grandparents.

It was surreal how perfect it felt, and for that moment, he almost wished it was real.

Meredith walked away to calm Sophie down and Cam let the fog of domestic bliss fade away.

This wasn't for him. Maybe someday, but even then there would be meals cooked in a stainless steel kitchen or served in the best restaurants. Cocktail parties. Business functions. A mandatory dinner with his parents at least once a week. If he was lucky, he and his someday family would have their own vacation place and he'd be able to join them on the occasional summer weekend.

As far as he could tell growing up, the Maguire summer house in the Hamptons was just a place his mother went to escape her husband and drink with her friends, which was easier if she left her son with a nanny and his father.

Cam didn't want that. He didn't want any of it, which was how he'd managed to avoid standing in front of an altar with all of his friends and family watching up to now.

Meredith appeared at his side a little while later and peered over his arm as he sliced into one of the steaks to check it. The close contact along with the heat from the grill made his face feel as if it were on fire, and he hoped if she noticed, she'd blame it on the flames. "I think I went a little past medium."

"They look great. You must be a natural."

It was a silly thing to be proud of, but her praise made him smile. "Let's hope these steaks taste as good as they look."

They did, and the macaroni salad Meredith and

her mother had whipped up was the perfect comple-
ment. While Elinor stared at them, obviously silently
judging them, from the other side of the glass slider,
they sat around Carolina's patio table—with a couple
of chairs borrowed from Meredith's and Sophie on
her grandfather's knee—and ate.

Cam didn't say a lot during dinner. The Lane-
Price family hadn't been together for a while and
they had a lot to catch up on. And if there was a lull
in the conversation, Sophie was quick to fill it.

He didn't mind. In fact, he preferred fading into
the background and watching this obviously loving
family interact. They clearly enjoyed each other's
company, and they laughed a lot. Maguire family
dinners were generally quiet and the small talk was
focused on business.

There was a vibrancy to Meredith that he'd seen
glimpses of, but surrounded by her family, her eyes
sparkled and her laughter came easily and often. He
watched her, idly sipping his lemonade, while he
pondered the mystery that was his neighbor.

She had money. That much was obvious from the
expensive SUV she drove, to say nothing of the lake
house she'd bought. And he wasn't much on fashion
or brand names, but he knew enough to know her
wardrobe would have her blending in with any of his
mother's social circles.

As a matter of fact, he could see her fitting in very

well in his world. Besides the surface polish—her hair, her nails and her clothes—the way she carried herself and spoke made him wonder if her husband had been somebody of note in business.

He forced himself to leave his phone in his pocket. He could do a Google search easily enough. Finding out who her husband had been would only take a few minutes. Hell, he could text his assistant and know pretty much everything there was to know about Meredith, her husband and everybody else in her family in a couple of days at most.

But this wasn't business. His relationship with her, such as it was, was strictly personal and for some reason it mattered to him. He didn't want a dossier. He wanted to get to know her, and for her to tell him things about her of her own accord.

Their eyes locked and when she tilted her head, the corner of her mouth quirked up in a half smile, he realized she'd caught him staring at her.

Rather than draw the attention of her parents by saying anything to her, he just smiled and turned his attention to Oscar, who was trying to beg a potato chip from Meredith's dad.

"We should hit the road," Neal said to Meredith when the light started changing and Sophie was clearly starting to drag. "Give you and my sweet granddaughter here some time to wind down before bedtime."

Cam glanced at his watch and was surprised by how quickly the afternoon had flown by. This was where he would generally take his leave so they could say their goodbyes in private, but they were on his deck. He wasn't sure he'd ever learned that etiquette lesson.

Fortunately, Meredith had it handled. "Yes, we should go back and get out of Cam's hair, anyway. Are you sure there's nothing else we can do to clean up?"

"I'm positive. Most of it was disposable, so there isn't much to do." And he didn't want an audience when he searched for YouTube videos teaching him to clean a gas grill.

He shook her parents' hands and told them how nice it was to meet them, and then rustled Sophie's hair. "I enjoyed the company today."

"So did I," Meredith said, giving him another of those genuine smiles that thrilled him. "Thank you for inviting us."

Once he was alone again, he filled the sink with hot soapy water to soak the few dishes they'd used and the greasy barbecue tools. Elinor sat regally on the back of the sofa, giving him a look of such intense disdain that a lesser man might have shriveled up in fear.

"Don't look at me like that," he told her. "They're

nice, and it doesn't hurt us to be neighborly once in a while."

In fact, he wouldn't have minded hanging out with them a little longer. He'd been missing the hustle and bustle of the city when he woke up that morning, so he'd driven over to the café for breakfast. It hadn't helped and a strong sense of loneliness had overcome him as he'd parked his car in the driveway.

Until he'd heard the hammock-induced laughter coming from his backyard. It had been a wonderful sound to return home to, even if it was temporary. Maybe someday he'd come home to the laughter of a wife and kids of his own, but if so, that was still a long way off.

Family had never been a particularly warm and fuzzy concept for him, so he'd never been in a hurry to replicate it and start his own. But if it could feel the way it had felt when he'd come home to Meredith and Sophie laughing in his backyard today, maybe there was hope for him, after all.

Chapter Five

A week later, Meredith walked out onto her dock and sat in the swing. Leaning her head back, she closed her eyes and inhaled deeply before blowing out a long, slow breath.

The move was officially over.

She'd had to order some cabinet and closet organizers and shelving units online, but all the stuff they owned had a place. Everything was unpacked. The last of the boxes had been broken down and put in the recycling bin.

Even with all of the downsizing they'd done before leaving California, she'd expected settling in to take longer than a week. A six-year-old and an energetic dog weren't exactly the best sidekicks for the project. But she'd made two lists each day—one for her and one for Sophie—and they'd tried to see who could check off all their tasks first. Meredith's jobs might have been more difficult, but it made her life easier when Sophie was engaged with her list.

Something landed on the swing beside her with a thump and Meredith opened her eyes just as Elinor climbed into her lap.

"Well, hello. Make yourself at home." She expected the cat to curl up on her lap, but Elinor only sat there, perched on her thighs, and stared at her. "Why do I get the feeling you're only sitting on me so you can cover me with cat hair, which will upset my dog when I go back inside?"

"That sounds about right."

The male voice definitely hadn't come from Elinor, and Meredith tried to ignore the little jolt of excitement as she turned to face Cam. She'd been so lost in thought she hadn't heard him approaching, and he'd probably come only to get his cat off her dock, but she couldn't deny there was a part of her that was happy to see him.

"I was trying to get to her before she could disturb you because you looked so peaceful out here, but she's pretty fast when she wants to be." He held up a small brown kibble of some sort. "And she doesn't seem to be as controlled by a desire for these treats as I'd hoped she'd be."

Elinor had been ignoring him, but she made a demanding mewling sound when he held up the treat. She didn't move, though, so it was clear she expected Cam to deliver it.

"If I give it to you now, I'll be rewarding you for jumping on the neighbor lady's lap while she was trying to take a nap in her swing."

"Not to interrupt this debate you're having with your cat, but I wasn't sleeping. Just taking a moment to enjoy being officially done with the moving process."

"She's not my cat," he muttered, but that didn't stop him from stepping forward and holding out the treat. Elinor still didn't move, so he had to lean close and feed it to her. Meredith tried not to laugh, but she couldn't hide her amusement. Cam shook his head. "I don't think I've ever met a living creature as stubborn as this cat, and that includes my father."

Once Elinor had finished her treat, Meredith stroked her fur. The cat arched her back against her hand, casting a "see, she does like me" look in Cam's direction. "I'm one hundred percent a dog person, but I *have* heard that about cats."

Cam chuckled and shoved his hands in his pockets. Meredith looked up at him, noticing the way the sun glinted off his hair before turning her gaze back to the cat. Over the last week, she and Sophie had spent more time inside than out in the yard, so she'd caught glimpses of her neighbor, but hadn't really spoken to him since the barbecue.

She'd heard him, though. A raised, angry voice on what seemed to be a business call that echoed out through the slider screen. A lot of attempts to find Elinor and bargaining to get her into the house so he could lock it up when he was going out or going to bed. Some hammering on the deck, followed by a word she had to make Sophie promise never to repeat.

"If she's bothering you, you can just pick her up and set her on the ground, you know," he said. "She'll only try it seven or eight more times before she finally gets the message and finds somebody else to harass."

"Probably Oscar."

"Probably." At least he looked a little apologetic about the fact his cat's favorite activity seemed to be appearing on the other side of a window or the slider to make Oscar bark.

"She's not bothering me," Meredith said. "She's a lot calmer than Oscar, who is currently curled up with Sophie in her bed because she's trying to teach him to read."

He laughed, and she wanted to wrap herself in the warm, vibrant sound. Sure, some aspects of having him as a neighbor got under her skin, and his cat liked to wind her dog up, but he really did have a great laugh.

"Do me a favor," he said. "If she successfully teaches him to read, make her promise she won't teach Elinor. She's enough of a handful as it is."

"How do you think she'll like New York City?"

His expression changed and she regretted asking the question. "I don't think she'd like my apartment at all. And there wouldn't be any going outside anymore. I'll probably start trying to find her a new home soon."

Meredith stroked the cat's fur, trying to imagine how upset she would be at leaving her cottage for a new home. Elinor had been Cam's grandmother's cat and she'd owned the cottage since before Meredith was born, so it was probably the only home Elinor had ever known.

"I don't need both of you looking at me like that," Cam said, his voice deep with annoyance. "She's not a city cat. I live in the city."

"It's none of my business," Meredith said, and then she sucked in a breath as Elinor leaped off her lap, since the process involved a little bit of claw. Not enough to pop through her shorts and draw blood, thankfully.

Cam scooped the cat up and sighed. "Sorry. I'm

just not sure what I'm going to do with her yet. Other than try to convince her to stay in her own yard."

"Maybe once I put a fence in, she'll get the hint."

"I don't think you can build a fence tall enough to keep her out when she's in a mood to annoy your dog."

He left then and, since there was no reason not to, Meredith allowed herself the pleasure of watching him walk away. There was a confidence to his stride—to everything he did really, except maybe grilling steaks—and she certainly liked the way he moved.

It was good, she thought, to feel the stirrings of desire again. She was young. She knew she would find love again, and finding a man attractive was a good start. Terrifying, too, since she'd been with Devin since college, but healthy.

Maybe if she was desiring somebody more suitable—like a man who actually lived in Blackberry Bay and wouldn't be running back to the city at the end of the summer—she'd more nervous about it. There was a big difference between being ready for physical attraction and being ready for an actual relationship, so quietly and secretly lusting after Cam was perfectly harmless.

With a sigh, she shoved herself up off the swing and walked back toward the house. Sophie was going to a puppet show at the library as part of their summer reading program and, if she knew her daughter, she was going to forget how excited she'd been and start dragging her heels. She liked the book parts a lot more than the social parts, but Meredith was sure she'd have a good time once she was there.

"Do you think there will be a lot of kids there?" Sophie asked once they were finally in the car and headed toward the library.

"I'm not sure, but it would be fun to meet new kids. Some of them will be your age and you can meet them before school starts." She was careful not to use the phrase "make friends" since that seemed to put even more social pressure on her daughter.

"I hope I like the school," Sophie said, and Meredith sighed. One worry at a time.

"I think you will. I loved it when I went there."

It took her a few minutes to find a place to park, so the program was getting ready to start as she found Sophie a good place to sit. "I'll be back before it's over, but you wait here in the children's section until you see me, okay?"

Sophie nodded, and then a musical introduction started. Another girl around Sophie's age smiled shyly at her, and when Meredith peeked around the corner a few minutes later to check that Sophie was doing okay, the two girls had moved their chairs closer together. She took that as her cue to leave.

She had an hour free and no idea what to do with

herself. There was a time she would have taken advantage of Sophie's social events to do errands that weren't child friendly, but in the last few months, she'd gotten used to her daughter doing everything with her. And they'd done all of their errands already, so it was literally a free hour.

With no destination in mind, she descended the library stairs and started walking.

Not having Sophie with her would have made it the perfect time to stop into the town hall and see what the rules were for putting up a fence, but after a quick search on her phone, she found out they were open from 9:00 a.m. to noon every other Saturday and today wasn't that Saturday.

Then she saw a sign that read Bishop's Auto Care & Bakery, and stopped in her tracks.

Reyna Bishop. There was a name she hadn't thought of in years. Reyna's dad owned the auto shop in town, and her mom had always been the star of the bake sale fund-raisers. At some point they must have combined their talents.

She could get a cupcake, and maybe find out if Reyna still lived in town. She wasn't sure how many of her old classmates would have stuck around after graduation or come back after college, but it was probably time to start finding out.

A small bell rang when she walked into the bakery, and the older woman behind the counter greeted her with a smile. "Good afternoon. What's your sweet tooth in the mood for today?"

"You probably don't remember me, Mrs. Bishop, but I went to school with Reyna. I'm Meredith Price now, but I was Meredith Lane then."

"Oh my goodness!" Mrs. Bishop shook her head, but she was grinning. "You've hardly changed at all! How are your parents doing? I've only seen your mom a few times since they moved out of town."

"They're well, but you'll probably see more of them now that I've moved *back* to town. I have a little girl who's six, so I don't think my mother will be staying away as much."

"Oh, you're the one who bought the house next to Carolina Archambault's cottage?" When Meredith nodded, she whistled through her teeth. "That's a beautiful house. I heard about your husband, though. I was sorry to hear it."

"Thank you." There was always a pang of grief when she talked about Devin, but they weren't as debilitating as they'd once been. "So how has Reyna been? Does she still live in town?"

"Oh, she's good. And she's working out in the garage right now, as a matter of fact. I lost my husband a few years back to cancer and she stepped in to help him out and never left."

"I'm so sorry, Mrs. Bishop. I didn't know." She knew how it felt to lose the man you thought you were going to spend the rest of your life with, but it didn't help her know the right words to say.

"I wouldn't have expected you to know, but thank you." Mrs. Bishop sighed and reached out to put her hand over Meredith's on the counter. "I'm doing okay, but I guess you know how it is. Some days are better than others."

She nodded for a few seconds because she wasn't sure if she could force words past the lump in her throat. Losing Devin had been a shock—her entire world changed in one phone call—but Mrs. Bishop had lost her husband slowly and she wasn't sure which would hurt more. But either way, they'd each suffered a devastating loss. "That's very true, though I have more better days than not now."

"And you've got your daughter to brighten your days."

"She's definitely a bright spot." Just thinking about her made Meredith smile, and Mrs. Bishop smiled, too. "Do you think Reyna would mind if I stopped in to say hi?"

"Of course she wouldn't. You can either go back outside and around to the shop door down back, or you can go through that door there and at the end of the hallway is a door into the shop office."

"I'll just go around," she said. "But I'll take a couple of those gigantic brownies there to save for dessert first."

Once she'd tucked the pastry bag into her tote and said goodbye to Mrs. Bishop, she went back outside and around the corner to the entrance to the auto part of their auto care and bakery endeavor.

The smell of oil and old engine parts greeted her when she walked into the office. To the left was a door she assumed led to the hallway back to the bakery. In front of her was a tall counter with a computer on it, as well as a stack of service slips. And to the right was a large garage door that was up, allowing her to see into the service bays.

"I'll be right there," a woman called, and a minute later Reyna walked into the office. She'd hardly changed at all, with a navy Bishop's T-shirt and stained jeans hugging a figure that had turned all the boys' heads in high school. Her thick reddish hair was up in a messy bun, and she had a smudge of grease on her cheek that did nothing to mar her beauty.

"Damn, Meredith Lane. How've you been?"

"Good. It's Meredith Price now, though."

"It's been a long time."

Reyna said the words matter-of-factly enough, but Meredith felt a rush of shame, nonetheless. It *had* been a long time since they'd spoken, even though they'd been really good friends all through school. But when Meredith had gone off to college, she'd gotten so wrapped up in her studies and building a new life in California that she'd just fallen out of touch with her friends in Blackberry Bay.

A lot of people looked up old friends and classmates on Facebook, but she'd never gotten around to it. She'd never thought about it, honestly. Her parents were always just a phone call away, and she'd let the rest of Blackberry Bay fade away. She'd signed up for the app only because it was how much of the information regarding Sophie's activities and friend groups was shared, and that was the extent of what she'd used it for.

Now, feeling the loss of an old friendship so keenly, she really wished she'd looked up Reyna and other friends and maybe reconnected, even if it was on the internet.

"I heard you were back," Reyna continued. "With a little girl?"

"Sophie's six. She's at the library right now for a summer reading program event, but hopefully I'll get to introduce her to you soon." She was fishing for encouragement and a little embarrassed by it, but she wanted a sign Reyna would be willing to pick up their friendship again, or at least be open to starting a new one.

"Sure, that sounds fun," Reyna said. "I'm pretty busy right now, but are you going to the fireworks next weekend, for the Fourth? Maybe we can meet up there?"

"That sounds great. I hadn't even thought about the Fourth yet. We used to have so much fun when we were kids." Blackberry Bay put on a great show for Independence Day.

They reminisced for a few minutes, laughing over shared childhood memories, including the time Hunter Fleck had smuggled some of his dad's cigarettes to the town square on fireworks night. He and his friends were smoking them in the bushes beyond the grandstand and the fire department, thinking the bushes had caught some random sparks from the fireworks display, had turned a low-pressure hose on them.

But when that story was over and silence started filling the office, Meredith felt compelled to fill it. "So, did you get married? Any kids?"

"Nope." Reyna sighed. "I don't have great luck with men, and I haven't been in a hurry to have children with any of them, so it's just me and Mom."

"I was sorry to hear about your dad. You run this shop alone now?"

"Yup. It wasn't exactly what I'd planned to do with my life, but it pays the bills and it makes me happy right now. Plus, Mom and I weren't ready to give it up." She shook her head and then smiled. "So let me give you my cell number and you can text me when you get to the park so we don't miss each other."

Meredith added Reyna as a contact in her phone and typed in the cell number as Reyna gave it to her.

Then she recited hers as Reyna copied it on a scratch pad next to her computer. "I'd put it right into my phone, but it's turned off right now thanks to a first date who wanted to bring me home to meet his mother after dinner."

"Ouch."

"Yeah, *ouch* is the official motto of my dating life so far."

"Well, I'll let you get back to work. But Sophie and I will definitely see you at the fireworks next weekend."

"Sounds great. It's good to see you again, Meredith."

She left the garage feeling lighter than she had in a long time. She'd had a lot of friends in California, of course, but they'd come to her through Devin's work or Sophie's social circle. Having a friend who knew *her* and with whom she had a shared history felt different.

The cherry on top of the good-day sundae was the smile on Sophie's face when the puppet show ended and she threw herself into Meredith's arms. "It was *so* fun, Mommy!"

"You can tell me all about it in the car, okay?"

And she did. As soon as Meredith's door closed, Sophie started talking. "Kiki is my new friend. Her name is Christina, but her baby brother called her Kiki before he could talk right and now everybody calls her that."

Meredith listened to her daughter chatter away all about Kiki and the puppet show, and smiled. It was good to see her daughter coming out of her shell again.

They both were, she thought as she pulled into the driveway and saw Cam leaning against his car with his arms folded, staring at his cottage.

"I'm going to tell Cam about the puppet show," Sophie said, and she was out of the car as soon as Meredith killed the engine.

She tried to call her back, but Sophie's excitement was so obvious, all she could do was laugh helplessly. It seemed like Cam had a way of charming *both* Price ladies.

"Cam!"

He sighed, knowing his train of thought was now derailed, and turned to face the girl sprinting toward him.

"Hey, Sophie. What have you been up to?"

What followed was a deluge of high-pitched words about puppets and a Kiki, and he could barely keep up with what she was talking about. But it had to do with the library and he knew how she felt about books, so he surmised Sophie had a really great afternoon.

"Do you have a library card?"

The abrupt silence after her question and the intense look she was pinning him with made it clear this was some kind of character test as far as she was concerned. "I don't have one, but I can put it on my list of things to do."

"My mom can help you," Sophie said earnestly, and he heard the choked-off sound of amusement her mother made. Meredith was behind him now, so he turned so he could see her on the other side of his car. "Mommy's good at getting library cards."

"I don't think I've ever had a library card, now that you mention it," he said, mostly in anticipation of Sophie's reaction.

She didn't disappoint. Her eyes widened and her mouth dropped open, hanging there for a few seconds before she shook her head. "You've never had a library card? Like…ever?"

"Not ever. I used the library at school and in college, but I've never had a town or city library card."

"That's very sad." The genuine sorrow for him in her eyes almost broke his heart.

"Maybe your mom will help me get one," he said, wanting Sophie's smile to light up her face again. Meanwhile, Meredith made the same face her daughter had a moment before—eyes wide and mouth open.

"She will!" Sophie faced Meredith, practically bouncing up and down on the toes of her tiny pink sneakers. "Mommy, you'll help Cam get a library card, right?"

Meredith shot Cam a look that should have set him on fire before smiling at her daughter. "Sophie, I'm sure Cam is perfectly capable of going to the library and getting a card."

"But he's never had one!"

Came enjoyed the way Meredith had to take a breath before plastering a smile on her face to answer her daughter. He also appreciated her not taking off a shoe and chucking at his head since he'd obviously put her in this position deliberately.

"If Cam needs my help getting a library card, then I'm sure Lisa will help him. Maybe doing paperwork is hard for him."

"Hey now," he protested, but Meredith only gave him a sweet smile.

Okay, maybe he deserved that, but he wasn't ready to surrender yet. "Maybe the next time you two go to the library, I can go with you to get a library card, and then I'll take you out for ice cream to celebrate."

Meredith's eyes narrowed, but Sophie was already jumping up and down, clapping her hands. "Please, Mommy? *Please?*"

Cam had made a critical error. He could see it in the way Meredith's spine straightened and her lips pressed together. In the game of Annoy Your Pretty Neighbor, he'd overstepped.

"We'll see," she said.

"You always say that, Mommy. *Please?* Cam needs a library card and you *love* ice cream. It's your favorite!"

"Okay," she said, followed by a deep sigh. "Yes, we'll do that. Now, you go inside and take Oscar to the backyard so he can go potty since he's been waiting for us. Make sure you clip his leash on and double-check it before you open the slider."

As soon as Sophie flashed him a triumphant grin and skipped into the house, he held up a hand. "Before you say anything, I'm sorry. I don't have any experience with kids and I didn't see the situation I was putting you in until it was too late."

She'd opened her mouth to speak—or more likely to verbally shred him—but she closed it again for a few seconds and then she nodded. "Thank you for that, since you didn't really give me a choice without breaking my daughter's heart. Using a child to manipulate her mother into a date is not cool."

It was his turn to start to speak and then not say anything right away. A *date*? He'd said he'd treat Meredith and Sophie to ice cream after a trip to the library. Was that really a date?

Based on his heart rate and the heat that flooded his body, he wasn't opposed to the idea of going on a date with Meredith. But the logical part of his brain knew getting involved with a widowed single mother was a bad idea, destined to be messy when he left at the end of the summer.

"I just wanted to push your buttons a little," he finally said. "And I thought Sophie might find a trip to the library and then ice cream exciting. She's cute when she's happy. It wasn't any more than that, but I'm still sorry."

"She's always cute. And she'll definitely love a day that includes books *and* ice cream." She smiled. "And so will I."

Crisis averted, he thought, relieved. "Hopefully the legal paperwork I have will be enough for them to give me a library card. I'm afraid Sophie might be tempted to storm the castle on my behalf if they decide I'm not enough of a resident."

She laughed. "She would definitely storm the castle if they denied you. But when I was a kid, they had summer cards for the lake people, so even if all the paperwork related to the house isn't officially in your name yet, you should be fine. And speaking of summer residents, why were you just hanging out, staring at the cottage, when I pulled in?"

He shrugged one shoulder. "Debating its curb appeal."

"It's certainly…eclectic."

"You say that like it's a bad thing."

"No, but if you're talking about curb appeal because you're going to put it on the market, people who can afford properties on the bay, especially with a private dock, generally aren't looking for eclectic."

He knew she was right, of course. But Carolina had loved this cottage. She'd fought for it, from the pink shingles to the disheveled wildflowers to the crooked flower boxes, and some part of him resisted homogenizing it to suit some mass real estate appeal.

"Honestly, it would be a teardown," she continued. "Somebody would buy it for the land, raze the cottage and build something new."

Oh hell no.

Cam prided himself on his business acuity. He might work for the family business, but he'd made his mark there. A lot of their recent growth had his name all over it. And he knew Meredith was telling him the truth, but he couldn't accept it.

Not yet, anyway. Maybe when he was finished reconciling himself to this alternative life he never got to experience, he'd be ready to let the cottage go without looking back, but he couldn't even consider it right now.

But Meredith wasn't done. "And that would raise the property values for all of the houses in the immediate area."

"You sound like a snob," he snapped before his brain could put the brakes on his mouth.

Her eyes widened. "Or a property owner who invested a lot of money in her home and cares to protect that investment."

"Maybe you should build that fence, after all." Before she could say anything else that would require a response from this strange and new defensive side of him, he turned and walked into the cottage.

They really did push each other's buttons, without even trying.

Okay, that wasn't true, he admitted to himself after a few minutes alone. He *had* been trying to push her buttons, even though it was on a subconscious level.

Maybe it was the way Carolina's love of her home had shone through in her journals, but he'd gotten defensive about Meredith's practical, logical observations and acted like a jerk.

He'd have to apologize, but for now he just wanted to be alone for a little while and try to get his head on straight.

This wasn't like him at all. Business was business and for any other comparable property, he would have been the first to suggest the best thing they could do for the property's value was tear down the cottage.

Being able to sleep without background noise and

making do without late-night food deliveries were normal adjustments to his new environment. But bringing sentimentality into a business transaction? That was so unlike him, he was almost afraid to look in the mirror.

It was a momentary weakness, he told himself. Khaki shorts and hammocks and pink cat mugs couldn't put a dent in one vital fact—Michael Archambault might be his biological father, but he was a Maguire.

And a Maguire wouldn't protect an old pink cottage because a woman he'd never met had loved it.

Chapter Six

It was Oscar's barking that woke Meredith before eight on Sunday morning, but under the frantic yips she could hear the annoying hum of a lawnmower.

A lawnmower that sounded so close that, as she threw back her covers, it seemed to pass right by her window.

Not okay, she thought as she crossed her room and peered through the curtains.

Cam was pushing one of the oldest lawnmowers she'd ever seen, seemingly oblivious to the smoke it was spewing and the obnoxious racket it was making at a barely decent hour.

She was still mad about what a jerk he'd been

about her very honest opinion that the property's curb appeal would be increased by tearing down the cottage. And its effect on *her* property value wasn't an opinion at all. That was a fact, even if she should have been more tactful about it.

And now this?

And Oscar needed to go out now, of course. Once he was up, there was no coaxing him back to bed. Because she hadn't gotten around to dealing with the fencing situation yet, she had to pull a cardigan on over her pajamas and snap the dog's leash on.

She glared at her neighbor's back—and the impressive shoulders hugged by his shirt—while she waited for Oscar to do his business. Cam pushed the mower in a straight line away from her, and she was still glaring at him when he turned.

Their eyes locked, and she concentrated on making sure everything from her facial expression to her body language conveyed how annoyed she was with him.

And she must have done a good job because he raised an eyebrow and then released the bar to allow the engine to sputter and die. Then he just waited.

"You have a cell phone and a smart watch, so I know you have ways of telling time," she said.

"Only if I look at them," he pointed out.

"There are ordinances about these kinds of things."

He folded his arms across his chest and tilted his head. "Are there?"

She was cornered and they both knew it. There were *probably* noise ordinances in Blackberry Bay, but she didn't know what they said. So she went a different direction. "You know, they make newer models of those. They're probably a lot more efficient. And quieter. They even make electric ones that are virtually silent."

"Why would I blow money on a new lawnmower when I have this trusty beauty?"

Beauty was a stretch. A *big* one. "I'm pretty sure a guy who can afford a car like yours can afford a new lawnmower with no problem."

He tilted his head, the amused quirk of his lips getting on her last nerve. "Maybe I can afford a car like that because I don't waste money replacing things that aren't broken."

Clearly she wasn't going to get anywhere with him before she'd had her coffee—although she wasn't sure even a full pot would be enough for Cam Maguire—so she turned on her heel and headed for the house. Luckily Oscar was ready to follow her without coaxing.

Once inside, she gave the dog a treat and had just decided to crawl back into bed when the lawnmower coughed a couple of times and roared to life.

She tried to tell herself it was for the best as she

prepared a mug of coffee and sat at the table to drink it. After Devin had died and the things that had filled their lives started slipping away, so had her sleep schedule. She'd started roaming the empty-feeling house at night. Napping during the day. It hadn't been healthy, but she hadn't been able to force herself to do better until she'd realized Sophie's sleep patterns were also being disrupted and kindergarten was around the corner.

It had taken months for Meredith to return to the structure of a healthy night's sleep, and even if she had trouble sleeping in a new house with new sounds around her, she needed to get up at a reasonable time so she could fall asleep at bedtime.

But eight o'clock on a Sunday was a perfectly reasonable time, so she had no intention of letting her inconsiderate neighbor off the hook. Who mowed their lawn that early on a Sunday morning?

Blackberry Bay almost certainly had noise ordinances that set out official quiet times because it was a town financially dependent on charming visitors and enticing them not only to stay but also to keep coming back. She should look into those while she looked into the requirements for installing a fence.

Sophie emerged from her bedroom, shuffling across the floor in unicorn slippers while rubbing her eyes. "Can we have heart pancakes today?"

"Good morning to you, too, sweetie." Meredith

pulled her up onto her lap and blew out a little breath as Sophie nestled against her and her daughter's dark blond hair tickled her face. "We can make heart pancakes today."

It hurt a little. Devin had started the habit of heart-shaped pancakes when Sophie was a toddler, and it was one of the strongest specific memories she had of her dad, so Meredith had kept it going. The memory of Devin and Sophie laughing together in the kitchen still made her heart ache, but she'd reached the place where it made her smile, too.

Once they'd had breakfast, Sophie went to get dressed with Oscar at her heels. Meredith was cleaning up when the lawnmower finally shut off for what she hoped was the last time for the day.

Then Cam moved into her field of vision and she totally forgot she was annoyed with him as he peeled off his shirt and blotted his forehead with it before flinging it over his shoulder.

His arms and torso weren't as tan as his hands and face, which made sense for a man who probably wore business suits every day before arriving in town. But he'd lost the tinge of pink, and she figured if he kept running around shirtless, the tan would even out in no time.

Watching him move around the yard wasn't a hardship, so she took her time hand washing the few dishes they used, telling herself there weren't enough to merit running the dishwasher.

Then he stretched out in his hammock, arms stretched up so he could rest his hands under his head, and she caught herself sighing like a teenage girl watching her crush.

And that was enough of that. She had things to do that didn't involve spying on her shirtless neighbor, no matter how good it felt to find herself lusting after a man again.

Elinor is not a fan of crutches or the cast on my foot. I'm not much of a fan, either, but somebody had to fix the roof and I didn't want to ask Michael. That boy is working himself to the bone, but he can't work through the kind of sadness he's carrying around with him. I try hard to be kind and find joy in the small things, but I'll hate that woman until the day I die. Maybe even longer if ghosts are real. I haven't really made up my mind about that.

Tess said I should hire someone, but I helped Thomas replace the roof years ago, so I thought I could fix such a little piece of it on my own. I should have listened to Tess. Michael said the same thing when he got to the hospital. And, of course, so did Tess. She might be my best friend, but that woman doesn't let go of anything.

So now Michael still had to fix my roof and I'm on crutches until my foot heals. At least it wasn't my hip. Finding joy in that small blessing.

Waking up at dawn after a fitful night's sleep hadn't exactly fit into the rest-and-relaxation thing Cam was going for this summer. And restlessly pacing around the small kitchen area didn't even come close to burning through the need for physical exertion he felt.

Going for a walk, or even a jog, didn't seem like enough, so he'd decided it was landscaping day and fired up the lawnmower. In retrospect, he should have looked at the clock first. Just because he'd been up for a while didn't mean everybody else in the neighborhood had.

But it hadn't dawned on him until he looked up and saw Meredith glaring at him as though she were daydreaming about knocking him over the head with one of his grandmother's terra-cotta flowerpots.

She was a beautiful woman, but when she was annoyed? She was stunning, he thought as he stripped off his sweaty clothes and turned on the shower. He knew from experience the water heater couldn't be much bigger than a coffee urn and that he shouldn't dawdle or he'd be washing the last of the soap off with cold water.

But with Meredith in his thoughts, maybe a cold shower wouldn't hurt.

In an effort to put his uncharacteristic reaction to Meredith—and the apology he owed her—out of his mind, he'd stayed up too late reading Carolina's journals, fascinated by the colorful personality of the woman who'd raised his birth father and how skilled she was at putting it on the page. And there were glimpses of his father in the journals. Not a lot, and he got the impression Michael Archambault hadn't been as devil-may-care as his mother, but Cam soaked up the details he could find, and it made it hard for him to put the books down.

Then, when he'd gone to bed, thoughts of Meredith had resurfaced and he'd done a lot of tossing and turning before he finally fell asleep.

After he'd finished mowing, he'd hit the hammock, determined to do Sunday-type things. He'd always known people tended to relax on the weekends, but that wasn't true in the Maguire household. While the offices were closed on Sundays, he and his father both had home offices that never closed.

He almost napped, but Sophie and Oscar playing in their yard kept him from actually nodding off. Meredith must have had a talk with her daughter because the little girl never called his name, and it sounded like she was playing with the dog on the far side of her yard.

As much as he needed to learn to totally relax, he was a little disappointed she didn't seek out his company. She was a fun distraction, and he'd never realized such small kids could have such big personalities. Maybe if he'd had siblings, he would have nieces and nephews to play with, but he was an only child and his social life was mostly business related. Acquaintances didn't bring kids to business lunches, cocktail parties or charity events.

He really needed to say he was sorry to Meredith, and not just for Sophie's sake. It bothered him that he'd upset Meredith enough that she'd told her daughter to leave him alone.

He'd had an opportunity when she laid into him about the lawnmower, but there was something about the way she looked when she was mad that made him want to challenge her—to keep pushing those buttons—instead of de-escalating the situation.

He should probably stop doing that if he wanted peace, but she was so sexy when she looked at him with those sparks in her eyes.

When Sophie and Oscar were called in for lunch, Cam decided that was a good idea, so he went inside and heated up a can of soup. His cooking skills were rudimentary at best, so he had a cabinet full of soup and a fridge well stocked with deli meats and cheeses. When all else failed, he could get by on soup and sandwiches. Now that he'd figured out the barbecue grill, he could probably add steaks and chicken breasts to his next shopping list, though.

Then he decided he could still count Sunday as a day off if he didn't do actual Maguire company business, so he spent the afternoon sifting through the plastic tote labeled Important Papers that Carolina had deemed sufficient for holding vital records and legal documents.

He scanned each paper as he pulled it out, and started spreading them across the table, trying to put them in order by year. And he was doing okay, seeing it as an exercise in organization, until he pulled out the death certificate for Michael Thomas Archambault, with his obituary paper-clipped behind it.

He'd been fifteen when his biological father passed away. He closed his eyes, remembering where he was when he was fifteen—at the boarding school where he was expected to learn discipline and make connections that would serve him in the business world. Mostly he'd learned detachment from his parents and made a couple of good friends he still spoke to on a regular basis while counting the days until he was an adult. His life might be tied to his father's forever, but he'd get his own apartment and make it his refuge.

Meanwhile, the man who was *actually* his father worked for a logging company and was killed in an accident.

> *Survived by his mother, Carolina Archambault, and a son, who was adopted by a loving family as an infant.*

Cam blinked, shocked to find tears blurring his vision. His grandmother had written that, he was sure. She'd felt compelled to include the grandchild she'd never seen when mourning the sudden loss of her son, and Cam's heart ached for her.

And for himself. This was *his* family, and he'd never gotten to know them. He hadn't gotten to play ball with his dad or help comfort his grandmother in her grief. His mother had robbed him of Carolina's warmth and love, and raised him in a cold household that prized success over all else.

Not surprisingly, he slept poorly that night, and his lingering anger carried him through his Monday-morning conference call with his father and other top executives in the company. Calvin III managed to make several references to his displeasure over Cam's working remotely, but he ignored them.

Then he spent the rest of the day putting out fires

from a distance, which involved a lot of computer time and several long phone calls. He was aware sometimes of the sounds from outside—it sounded like Meredith and Sophie were gardening—and Elinor came and went through the cat door, but mostly it was a day to put his head down and work.

His mother called shortly after he finished the cold turkey sandwich he was calling his dinner. He didn't want to answer it, but there was no point in sending her to voice mail. If she had something to say, she wasn't going to be put off, and he reminded himself that at the end of the summer, he was going back to her world.

"Your father called me a few minutes ago," she said once the standard greetings were out of the way. "He's displeased with you."

He's displeased with you. There was a time avoiding hearing those words drove every decision he made. Not so much anymore. "I'm sorry to hear that."

"He feels your little vacation is happening at an inconvenient time."

Calvin III often filtered his displeasure through his wife, as if parental lectures were somehow more palatable to Cam coming from his mother. And it kept Cam's responses in check, because he obviously couldn't have a shouting match with her.

"First, I'm not on vacation. I'm working remotely,

and accomplishing what I need to accomplish. Second, I've never actually taken a vacation because there's never a convenient time, so if I *was* on vacation, which I'm not, I'd have earned it."

"Why can't you spend weekends with this woman and her family and weekdays in the office?"

It took Cam a few seconds to remember that his mom didn't know he was in Blackberry Bay. She didn't know he was sifting through her secrets and lies, trying to piece together a picture of the life he didn't grow up in.

"Traveling that much would result in more lost work time than simply working remotely. I'll come back to the city for a couple of days next week and then again in August to deal with any matters requiring my actual presence. Considering how seldom I leave my office, it doesn't really matter where that office is."

And they weren't going to find out where it was. He'd spent almost an hour before the first video conference with his father to ensure his webcam caught nothing but a blank wall as background behind his head.

His mother sighed. Not the affectionate, weary sigh he'd heard from Meredith with Sophie, but a sharp sound that indicated she wasn't getting her way and she wasn't happy about that.

"Who *is* this woman you're seeing, anyway?"

she snapped, since Cam clearly wasn't going to be swayed by his father's displeasure. "I've heard nothing about her, and it's foolish that she and her family think you can just go and stay for the summer like this. Especially since we haven't met her yet, which is just rude."

"They think I can go away for the summer because that's just what I'm doing, and I'll introduce her to you when I'm sure she's going to be a part of the family," he lied smoothly. "And spending the summer together is something their family has always done. It's a big lodge, with several wings. But there are also several rooms that serve as remote offices for those who need them."

"I've never heard of anything so ridiculous."

In hindsight, he probably should have come up with a better cover story to explain a prolonged absence. But he couldn't claim business overseas or anything else professional, since his father knew everything that went on with the Maguire holdings. So he'd been left with a personal excuse and, still reeling from receiving the letter from Carolina's lawyer, it had been the best he could come up with.

"We'll have dinner when you come home next week," she said firmly. "You should bring the woman so we can at least meet her."

The woman. Most mothers would have been excited for him and asking to meet his girlfriend, or at least have asked her name. Maybe even thinking ahead to weddings and grandbabies. But not his mom. She just didn't like having question marks in her son's life that could affect the business. If it had an impact on the company, her husband would be upset, and nobody liked that.

Another reason he hadn't been in a hurry to settle down. The idea of bringing a woman home to present to his parents for judging made his stomach turn.

"I'm meeting Claudine for dinner tonight," she continued, without waiting for his answer to her summons. "So I'll have to let you go if I don't want to be late. Send me your travel plans when they're made so I can make a reservation."

Calls with his mother just sort of ended once she'd decided she'd had the last word, so Cam said goodbye to dead air before dropping the phone on the table. Elinor hopped up to sniff at it, and then she tried to shove it off the edge. As much as he agreed with her sentiment, it was an expensive phone and he wasn't sure he could get a same-day replacement in Blackberry Bay, so he caught it before it could tip off onto the floor.

"You'd probably like my mother," he told the cat. "You're both stubborn, opinionated and very bossy."

Elinor just stared at him, blinking occasionally, until Cam closed his laptop. Eating in front of it was a bad habit, but there was no desk in the cottage.

Eating at the table made eating while working too easy, and he was going to have to be more disciplined about it if he didn't want buying a new wardrobe in a size up to be in his near future.

"What do you say we put a movie on and just forget about the rest of the world for a while?"

She didn't answer, of course, but once he'd cleaned up and stretched out on the sofa to surf through the television channels, Elinor curled up on his stomach and purred.

It was nice, he thought. For now. She was going to feel very heavy after a bit, and he could only hope she didn't start doing that kneading thing she liked to do with her claws, but for a while he was just going to lose himself in the TV and enjoy Elinor's company.

It was amazing how easily he'd put his mother's call out of his mind, he thought as he settled on a disaster movie he'd seen once before. Volcanic eruptions were entertaining, at least.

Usually his mother's displeasure made him tense—sometimes so tense it crept up his neck and became a headache he couldn't shake—but it was hard to be tense wearing shorts and a T-shirt, stretched out on the couch before the sun even went down.

Maybe it was the cat, he thought, reaching up to scratch the one spot on the side of her neck he'd found that didn't make her try to shred his hand.

Pets had never been a consideration in the Maguire household. They were messy. They took time and attention away from important things.

He couldn't help but wonder if they felt the same way about children.

But he was starting to understand why people loved having animals in their homes. There was something about the way you just had to take care of their basic needs and give them affection, and in return they adored you. No stress. No demands. No judgment. They just wanted to hang out and cuddle. Even Elinor, though he wasn't sure she quite adored him. But she was always willing to allow him to scratch that spot on her neck when he needed company.

Or maybe it was Blackberry Bay. Life had a different rhythm in the small lakefront town, and it had been jarring at first. But there was definitely something to be said for hammocks and lemonade by the water.

Chapter Seven

On Tuesday afternoon, Meredith took a deep breath and knocked on the front door of Cam's cottage. It probably would have made more sense to go to the slider, but that felt weird to her. She'd be able to see into the cottage before he knew she was there, and she still felt guilty enough about watching him in the yard on Sunday.

She hadn't seen him outside since. Elinor had been over a few times to annoy Oscar, but Cam must have been keeping himself busy indoors. And she wouldn't interrupt his work or whatever he was doing, but Sophie hadn't forgotten Cam didn't have a library card and she wasn't letting it go.

He pulled open the door while barking into his phone, and she would have waved him off and come back later, but he pushed open the wooden screen door and gestured with his head for her to come in. Then he held up a finger to let her know he was almost done.

"Yes, I expect you to know there's an impending divorce and asset division before acquisition," he was saying. "That's why we employ investigators."

Meredith had experience with waiting for a business call to wrap up, thanks to her marriage, so she tuned him out and looked around.

This was definitely not the kind of environment she'd ever imagine Cam being in. Everything was clean and fairly tidy, so she didn't think his grandmother had been hoarding, but she definitely owned a lot of *things* and the cottage was not very big. And the decorating scheme—which included an over-abundance of items stitched, quilted, knit and painted by hand—was decidedly feminine.

There were also cardboard boxes everywhere, in various states of being filled. She could see one with yarn in it, and another with papers. Embroidery thread. It was obvious he was trying to sort through Carolina's belongings, but there was a lot to sort. And he was going to need a lot more boxes.

"Sorry about that," he said, tossing the phone onto a round table covered with a laptop, a black leather folio and a white tablecloth decorated with Chihuahuas wearing Santa hats.

"That's quite a tablecloth," she said, because it was impossible to leave it unremarked upon. "Especially for June."

"There are no words for it, really. I was going to throw it away, but Elinor sat in the middle of the table and refused to move, so I gave up. Sorry about the mess everywhere. Do you want to sit? I have… water. Or coffee. All I have left in the house is coffee, water and a few slices of ham."

"I'm fine, thank you. Do you have people who grocery shop for you at home?"

"No, I don't," he said, gesturing to a chair that didn't have a box on it. "I mostly have business dinners in restaurants or have food delivered to the office or my apartment. That's apparently not a thing in Blackberry Bay, so I'm learning to feed myself."

She sat where he pointed, and waited while he moved a box so he could sit. "I'm sorry to barge in like this, but Sophie's being a little much right now."

"So you abandoned her to Oscar's care and you're going into hiding over here?"

The grin he gave her made her laugh. "Trust me, it's tempting. But I left her video chatting with my mother so I could talk to you about the library."

"Weren't you just there on Saturday?"

"Yes, and since she gets to have ice cream with

you the next time she goes, she's already read every book she checked out on Saturday. Watching her was like a master class in speed-reading."

"I didn't think kids that little were so smart."

She chuckled. "If you hadn't already told me you don't have experience with children, that statement right there would be enough to give you away. They're evil geniuses in training from the time they're born."

"When do you want to go?"

Part of her had braced herself for Cam begging off. Whether he had too much work or some other excuse, she'd assumed he'd regret setting up a library and ice-cream outing with her. Or maybe he'd still be feeling salty about their curb appeal conversation.

"I wasn't sure you were still on board," she confessed.

"I've had a lot going on with an acquisition going south and when I've seen you through the window, you've had Sophie with you. But I wanted to talk to you alone so I could apologize for the other night. I was a jerk and I don't have an excuse for it, so I'm sorry."

"I'm sorry, too."

"You don't have anything to be sorry for. You were right in your assessment and I called you a snob."

"Sometimes, if it's somebody's home, assessments can be delivered with a little more grace," she said, and when he smiled, she returned the smile. She was happy to put that behind them. "So you're still in for a trip to the library?"

"There's no way I could look that little girl in the face and tell her no. Plus, I'm a pretty big fan of ice cream."

"I know you have work to do along with doing all of…this."

"To be honest, I could use a break from going through her stuff. It's pretty overwhelming."

"There's nobody else helping? Any other family?"

"No." He was quiet for a long moment and then he looked her in the eye. "I didn't know about Carolina until after she passed. Her only child was my biological father, but I didn't know about him, either, and he passed away before she did. I was conceived during a brief separation in my parents' marriage and my mother chose to return to the man I know as my father. So there's nobody else. I got a letter from her attorney telling me I inherited this cottage from a woman I'd never heard of and that her cat was waiting for me at the local shelter."

"Oh." For a long moment, she didn't have any idea of what to say. It was a lot to process, and she couldn't even imagine how hard it must be on him. "I'm sorry. That's quite a bit to handle."

"I could have had it dealt with, of course. I certainly didn't have to come out here for the summer, but I was curious about her. About my real father, too—his name was Michael—so I wanted answers. So here I am with a cat who's not mine and a whole lot of…stuff."

She smiled, because as far as she was concerned, the fact he'd picked up the cat and brought her home even though he had no desire for a pet said a lot about him. "You sound like a man who needs to eat ice cream with a six-year-old who's celebrating your first library card."

His return smile was slow but genuine, crinkling his eyes. "That sounds perfect, actually. When should we go?"

"Whenever works for you. We're pretty open, but I'll repeat that she read all of her current books as fast as possible because she's that excited."

"How about tomorrow, after lunch? Even if I wrap up everything I need to do today, my head's going to be caught up in the acquisition and I'd rather save it for a fresh day."

"Tomorrow sounds great." It was on the tip of her tongue to invite him for dinner, seeing as how all he had was coffee and a little ham, but something held her back. One, he was a grown man. He could figure out how to feed himself. And two…some part of her still needed some distance between them.

Dealing with that tingle of anticipation when she was going to see him was hard enough. Managing just how far her imagination went when she caught sight of him working in the yard was even more challenging. The three of them around her table, laughing and sharing a meal, was too much right now.

At least the ice-cream date had been his idea and accepting it had been Sophie's doing. Meredith could still pretend she had no interest in her temporary neighbor, other than trying to be friendly.

She stood, since she'd accomplished what she'd come here for. And she could leave her mother video chatting with Sophie for only a few minutes because it was exhausting, even for a loving grandmother. "I don't really remember Mrs. Archambault or her son very well. I wish I did. But I *think* she was friends with Mrs. Weaver, who was the mother of one of my friends before I left. It's a small town, so if you ask around, you might find out a lot."

"I will at some point," he said. "I was going to ask your parents if they knew her, actually, but then I didn't. My parents don't know I'm here. They don't even know that I know about Michael, so I guess I'm just afraid of somebody saying something to the wrong person or on social media. My family tends to fly under the media radar as a rule, outside the business pages, but something like this would make headlines."

"That makes me curious about your family. Devin

did most of his business in Southern California and your last name doesn't ring any bells for me."

"If you do a Google search, you'll just get business articles, a few photos of my father and me in suits, and shots of my mother at various charity functions. I'd rather not spice up the results with a paternity scandal."

Her face flushed, because she'd already done that—she did a basic search on any adult who would be around Sophie on a regular basis—and that was exactly what she'd found. She'd also noticed he didn't resemble his parents very much, and now she knew why. "I understand. But let me know if you decide you'd like to reach out to people. I've been gone a long time, but I'm still from here. And, in the meantime, Sophie and I can help you sort through things."

"I couldn't ask that of you. There's so much stuff here."

"Which is why you need help." And there went her resolution to keep some distance between them. "You can take your laptop into the bedroom or out onto the deck, and Sophie and I can sort yarn and paint and whatever else is going on. Just an hour a day or so would make more of a dent than you'd imagine. Think about it."

"I will. And I really appreciate it." He walked her to the door. "Tell Sophie I'm excited about my library card, okay?"

"I will. And we'll be ready anytime after lunch, so just let us know when you're ready to go."

She was halfway down the walk when he called her name. She turned, and he was still in the open doorway, watching her.

"I really am sorry I called you a snob," he said, grinning.

"I was *being* a snob and I'm sorry I insulted your curb appeal. The plastic flowers in the window boxes are really going to cheer up the neighborhood come February."

He was laughing when he closed the door, and she was still smiling when she walked through hers.

"Do you think I should laminate it?"

Sophie frowned at the library card Cam held up. "I don't know what that means."

"Putting plastic on it so it doesn't get ruined if I get it wet."

"Why would your library card get wet?"

"What if I knock over a drink on the table and it spills on my card?"

The lines between Sophie's eyes deepened. "Why would your library card be on the table while you're having a drink?"

"I guess that's a good question," Cam said, admitting defeat. "Maybe I should just keep it in my wallet, where it'll be safe."

"And you won't lose it," she added, with all the wisdom of a seasoned library card holder.

Meredith chuckled as Cam tucked his pristine new card in his wallet for safekeeping, and Sophie nodded her approval.

"Should we go back to the cars before we go have ice cream?" he asked, and he winked at Sophie. "I don't want to drip on my books."

"You have to lick around the edges so it won't drip, silly."

They did go back to their cars, though, which were parked side by side in the municipal lot. Meredith had looked uncertain when Sophie asked if they were all going to ride together, so Cam had suggested he take his own car so he could go to the market after.

Once their books—along with the Spurr Memorial Library tote Sophie had talked him into buying and the documentation he'd brought to prove his residency for now—were locked in their cars, they walked down the main street to one of several ice-cream shops.

Sophie walked between them, chattering about how excited she was for the next summer reading program event because she'd get to see her friend Kiki again, and Cam was content to listen.

It was nice, he thought. Maybe too nice, since this wasn't actually his family he was sharing this typical family outing with, but he chose not to think too hard about it. He'd just enjoy the company while he had it.

They all ordered twist soft-serve ice cream in a cone, and as they walked to the park behind the shop and found a shady spot in the grass, Sophie showed him how to lick around the edges to keep it from dripping down his hand.

It still dripped. So did Sophie's, despite her expertise, and Meredith was the only one who managed to eat her entire ice cream without getting sticky hands. Luckily, she had packets of wet wipes in her bag and he cleaned his hands while she cleaned Sophie's.

"Mom, that's Robbie. He was at the puppet show. Can I go say hi?"

Cam looked to where Sophie was pointing and saw a couple of women sitting on a bench talking while two boys about her age threw rocks into the bay. It was a little close to the water for his taste, but Meredith nodded.

"You can talk to them, but don't go any farther. And be careful of the water."

"Can she swim?" he asked when Sophie had moved out of earshot, and the concern he heard in his own voice made him wonder who he was anymore. Powerful and successful Cam Maguire fretting about a child playing too close to the water.

"She's a good swimmer and she's careful." Meredith chuckled. "Not that I won't be keeping an eye on her, but I want to encourage her to make new friends. I was surprised she took to you so easily, actually. She can be really shy with strangers."

"I'm pretty sure it was my hammock," he teased. "She realized how fun it would be to read a book in it and forgot to be shy."

She laughed. "You're probably right about that."

"Tell me about her dad." He realized as soon as he voiced the thought that it sounded abrupt and maybe even rude, but she didn't look offended.

"Why?"

"I'm just curious. She's such a great kid and there's this whole part of her life I know nothing about." He turned away from the water then, his gaze locking with hers. "A whole part of your life I know nothing about. But if you don't want to talk about him, I understand."

"No, I..." She sighed. "I should talk about him more. I don't want Sophie to ever feel like we'll forget him. Devin was a very busy man—he was a hugely successful venture capitalist—but when he was with us, he made sure he was present. He was a very loving dad. And husband."

"I'm glad. You both deserve that."

She nodded, but he could see she was blinking away tears. "We were always busy. His work. Dinners. Charity things. Sophie had activities and playgroups and then school. It felt like we always moved a hundred miles per hour, but when it was family time, nothing intruded on that. Then when he died…"

His hand covered hers and she didn't pull away from the comforting gesture. "I'm sorry."

"No, I'm fine. We were busy at first, but then things—and people, unfortunately—started falling away and it was just Sophie and me rattling around in this empty shell of what used to be a very full life."

"Is that why you moved back here?"

"Mostly. Also, my parents. But we needed a Meredith-and-Sophie-sized life to be happy in."

"And how's it fitting?"

She smiled. "We're definitely happier here. I feel like it was the right decision."

"Have you thought about what you're going to do when she starts school? I mean, not to be nosy, but I noticed you stay home with her."

"I told myself I'd figure it out after the move, so I'll have to start thinking about it soon. I finished college—four years of business administration, which I switched to when I realized art history was a passing interest and not my calling—but I married Devin and never used it, other than helping him out in the office when work was hectic."

"Free office help," he said, and then he chuckled. "Lucky man."

It wasn't until she withdrew her hand that he realized he'd still had his resting on it. Not holding her hand, exactly, but close. "He was. I was a lucky woman."

"I didn't mean anything by that."

"I know, and like I said, it's good to talk about him." She pulled her knees up and wrapped her arms around them. "And I was very lucky that Devin was a financial whiz who liked to plan for the worst, so I don't actually *have* to work. But, like you said, Sophie's going to start school and I have to do something with my time. Taking the summer with her has been amazing, but it's not in my nature to sit around, doing nothing."

"Maybe you could buy Carolina's cottage and be the owner of an instant secondhand store and a cat."

She laughed, as he'd hoped she would. "Oh no, you don't. I told you I'd help you sort yarn, *not* take the entire thing off your hands. Why? Are you in a hurry to get back to the city?"

"No, not really."

Not at all, despite his expectation when he arrived that he would be able to get his answers, close out the estate and get back to New York City as soon as possible. Despite the lack of grocery delivery or restaurant options at midnight. Despite his parents' displeasure and not being on-site at the office.

The last thing he felt right now was a sense of urgency to get back to the life he'd put on pause.

He wanted more of this. Sitting in the park with

Meredith, watching Sophie play. More people who wanted to talk to him about something other than profits and losses—who seemed to actually enjoy his company. More sunshine on his face and clear blue water to look out over. More days not wearing a tie.

Cam glanced over and caught Meredith looking at him. Their gazes met and held for a few seconds, and she smiled before turning her attention back to Sophie, who was laughing with the other kids.

Warmth that had nothing to do with the sun flooded through him, and he didn't stop smiling after Meredith looked away. That life—the lonely, stress-filled life he'd been born into—could wait. Right now, he had more important things to do.

Chapter Eight

Meredith pulled open the door of the Cedar Street Café and stepped inside, hoping the noise of the crowd would drown out the sound of her stomach growling. She was starving and, after dropping Sophie—who'd eaten her breakfast in the car after they had an alarm malfunction—at the library, she'd decided to grab something in town.

The library hosted a lot of summer reading program events, which was awesome, but Sophie didn't accept that they were intended to be a pick-and-choose situation. She wanted to do them all, even a morning craft session.

She walked to the counter, intending to take a seat

there, when she heard her name. A tall brunette was walking toward her, an apron bearing the café's logo tied around her waist, and it took Meredith a moment to place the woman.

"Rissa? Oh my goodness, it's been ages!" Clarissa Shaw had been a couple of years ahead of her and Reyna in school, but their social circles had overlapped sometimes. While they hadn't been super close, they'd been friendly growing up.

After a brief hug, Rissa stepped back. "I heard you were back. I've been hoping you'd stop in."

"Do you work here?"

She laughed. "I work here a *lot*. My husband and I bought it five years ago."

"And you run it together?"

"We did, until he took off for greener pastures. Now it's all mine, which is good, but it also keeps me busy." Rissa held up a finger to a customer who called her name, and then gave Meredith an apologetic look. "Sit wherever you want, but I've got to get Bob more coffee before he gets up and tries to pour it himself."

After glancing down the counter, she saw another familiar face and her pulse quickened.

Cam was sitting on the stool at the far end, sipping coffee as he read something in front of him on the counter. And while she was frozen, trying to decide if she should sit down next to him or walk out the door, he turned and looked right at her.

The way his expression softened when he saw her and his lips curved into a smile had her moving toward him.

The way he closed the book and set it on the other side of his plate was a clear invitation to sit on the stool next to him, so she did. "Good morning. I didn't expect to see you here."

They'd been in such a rush to get to the library, she hadn't even noticed his car wasn't in his driveway. And she hadn't noticed it on the street when she was parking, either.

"I thought it would do me good to get out of the house for a bit. Also, I'm out of bread." They laughed, and then he waited while Rissa stopped by to take Meredith's order.

"Doing some reading?"

"Yeah." He rested his hand on the book, which she could see was a hardcover notebook with a tattered ribbon hanging from the bottom. "Reading Carolina's journals has been interesting, to say the least. They're not organized in any way, so I'm reading things in random order. She also adds memories in here and there, so even in one book, there's not a lot of chronological order."

"Just from the cottage, I can guess she was probably an interesting woman."

He chuckled, and she thought she heard genuine affection in it. "That she was. Which reminds me, I need to tell Sophie how Elinor got her name."

"It's in the journal?"

He nodded. "I came across that part yesterday. I guess her friend Mary rescued a cat and then found out she was allergic to cats. Carolina was alone, since this was after my—after Michael died, so she offered to take her. Mary named her Elinor after a character in her favorite book. One of Jane Austen's, I guess."

"Sense and Sensibility?" she asked, unsure because it had been years since she'd read Austen.

"That's the one. I think Sophie will be happy to know Elinor got her name from a book."

"She's going to love that." Meredith fixed the coffee Rissa set down in front of her, and then glanced at the journal. "There's so much to learn about Carolina. They're a treasure."

"The more I read them, the more I wish I'd gotten to know her."

The regret was heavy in his voice and she covered his hand with hers. "It's sad that you never got to meet her, but at least you're reading these, so she's still remembered."

He nodded and then cleared his throat. "Yeah. So what brings you in this morning? I mean, besides the obvious. Where's Sophie?"

"This might come as a huge surprise, but she's at

the library." They laughed, and she tried not to pay attention to Rissa giving them a curious look from the other end of the counter. "Another summer reading program thing, and we overslept, so it was kind of a mad dash out the door. She had a granola bar and some fruit in the car, but I was starving. The food was always good here."

"It still is," he said, gesturing to his empty plate, which he'd pushed away to make room for Carolina's book. "I swear, I'd eat here every morning if I wasn't already slacking off of work more than I should be."

"You don't have to keep me company if you need to get back."

He shook his head. "I'd rather sit and talk to you, if you don't mind."

"Of course I don't mind." It was ridiculous how much she didn't mind, and she lifted her coffee mug to her lips, hoping the steam would explain the heat she felt in her cheeks. "How does your father feel about you slacking off of work?"

He snorted. "I haven't actually slacked off enough so he'd notice, since I'm still getting the must-do things done. But compared to my usual hours, I *feel* like I'm dropping the ball."

"It good to relax now and then. You have to recharge your batteries, you know. And it's hard to resist hammocks. And playing catch with cute dogs. And we both know Sophie is a big distraction."

"She's the best kind of distraction," he said, and Meredith melted a little inside. "And don't forget Elinor. She has no problem plopping herself on my laptop keyboard if she decides it's time to take a break."

"I've heard cats like the heat from laptops."

"Yeah, but when her butt deletes an email draft, it's a problem."

"At least her butt didn't send the email draft." She laughed when he cringed at the thought. "Have you tried putting an empty box on the table near the laptop?"

"Why would I do that?"

She laughed again. "You really don't know anything about cats, do you?"

Rissa arrived with her breakfast and topped off both cups of coffee. It looked as if she was going to linger for a minute and chat, but then somebody called her name from the kitchen and she sighed before giving Meredith an apologetic smile and walking away.

Now that she knew Rissa owned the café, she'd have to stop in more often. Maybe she and Reyna could meet up for coffee during a slow time and visit. But for now, she didn't mind. She had Cam to talk to.

A mother knows things about her child. Michael hasn't told me yet, but I think he might be falling in love.

Tess said there's been talk around town about him helping a woman who got a flat tire when she was leaving one of those ridiculous parties the summer people like to throw. What kind of people have a backyard barbecue catered?

People with too much money, that's who. And people who have too much money usually get up to no good because they surround themselves with people who don't tell them no.

But Michael has been seen going in and out of the inn several times, even though he really has no business there. And Tess told me her car was in the parking lot for a few days, even though she'd been on her way out of town when she got the flat tire.

And now her car's in the lot behind his apartment.

I want Michael to fall in love and start a family. All of my friends have grandchildren and I want it to be my turn. But I don't feel like any good can come from him getting involved with one of the summer people.

Maybe I'm being unfair to her. Just because she has a fancy car and has friends with lake houses doesn't make her a bad person. But it means she has a whole different life

*than Michael, and she certainly won't want
to stay in his.*

   *Maybe it's wrong for a mother to say, but I
hope it's just a casual fling.*

A persistent sound from his open laptop jerked
Cam out of the past, and he closed Carolina's journal with a thump that startled Elinor.

When he realized his father was trying to video
chat with him, he glanced over his shoulder to make
sure the background was clear before adjusting the
camera angle and accepting the call.

Calvin III's face appeared on his screen, but Cam
was still thinking about how his mother crossed
paths with Michael, so he just stared at his father
for a long moment.

Too long a moment, judging by his father's scowl.
"Are you there? Did the screen freeze?"

Cam shook his head. "No, I'm here."

"We have a problem."

So many calls from his father had started that
way over the years, Cam didn't feel even the faint
stirrings of alarm. "Tell me what it is so we can
solve it."

When Calvin III started talking, he paid attention
for the most part, though he was very conscious of
the journal sitting off to the right of the laptop.

So his mother had visited friends who happened

to be summering in Blackberry Bay and a guy helped her change a flat and…she just stayed? Had Michael been that charismatic? Walking away from everything being a Maguire meant for a romance with some blue-collar guy would be incomprehensible to the woman who'd raised him.

He'd asked Carolina's lawyer if Michael had ever married. He already knew he hadn't fathered any other children, but that didn't mean he hadn't fallen in love and married somebody else.

But he hadn't. The lawyer told him from what he'd heard, Michael had been one of those guys who seemed content to be a bachelor for life.

"Are you paying attention?" his father snapped.

"Of course," he snapped back.

Elinor chose that moment to inform Cam it was time to stop working and, because he was so focused on the screen, he didn't see her coming in time to stop her.

She walked between him and the laptop, stopping to arch her back and butt her head against his chin.

"Is that a cat?"

"Yes. Her name is Elinor."

"They have a cat named Elinor?"

It took Cam a few seconds to remember that they were all pretending he was staying with a girlfriend's family for the summer. "Yes, and she can be rather persistent, I'm afraid."

He risked the wrath of her claws by picking her up and setting her on the floor. When she crouched, obviously intending to jump back onto the table, he put out his hand in a *stop* command. She glared at him, but then she must have decided he wasn't worth the effort.

He'd probably pay for that later.

"Okay," he said, turning his full attention back to his laptop. "You were saying?"

He was more focused this time, especially when his father brought up the possibility an employee they'd trusted for a long time might be embezzling from them. It was a substantial amount of money, and Cam was tasked with gathering the necessary evidence that would either prove or disprove the man's guilt.

Cam hoped they were wrong. It was hard enough to trust people in business without your own people betraying you.

"Needless to say, we want to handle this as quickly and quietly as possible," his father was saying. "Not only do we not want him to know we're looking at him, but we want to protect the stock prices."

"Understood," Cam said, since he wasn't hearing anything he didn't already know. Maybe Calvin III didn't hug him as a child, but he'd taught him how to stay on top in the business world.

"Is there anything else we need to discuss?" his

father asked, and Cam locked eyes with him on the screen.

Yes. How many zeroes were on the check you wrote to Michael Archambault? What was his price for giving me away? Did he negotiate at all or just take the first offer you put in front of him?

How much was I worth to him? To you?

"No," he said. "Nothing else."

He could demand answers, he thought as they disconnected the chat. He could probably get his father to tell him everything. But he didn't need to know the answer to that question. His worth didn't come from a dollar amount.

He wanted to know how a man could give up his child, and the amount on the check wouldn't give him that answer. And his father wouldn't be able to give him that answer.

He could only hope that Carolina's journals would.

Chapter Nine

"This is a good spot, Mommy."

It was as good a spot as any, and since they'd spent the last twenty minutes wandering through the maze of families in the park, Meredith was well past being picky about it.

It had taken forever, too, since a lot more people in Blackberry Bay remembered her than she would have guessed, and making their way through the maze had included at least a dozen stops to say hello.

"Help me spread the blanket out, then," she said, dropping the quilt she'd been carrying around for the better part of an hour.

Once they'd spread it out and felt around for any

rocks under the fabric, she had to admit Sophie *had* chosen a good spot. They'd have a perfect view of the fireworks show over the bay, and there was enough room so people could walk around their quilt instead of over it, while not leaving enough room for people to spread more blankets next to them.

The downside to getting a good spot, of course, was being there early and having time to kill before the show started. She unzipped the outer pocket of the backpack she'd prepared for tonight and took out her cell phone. The first text she sent was to her parents, who were meeting them there, so they'd know where to look for them.

Then she sent a text to Reyna. If you get a chance to stop by, Sophie and I parked our quilt about halfway between the gazebo and the big maple.

They weren't the most precise directions, but if Reyna wandered in their direction, she'd find them easily enough.

"When are Grandpa and Grandma coming?" Sophie asked for the umpteenth time.

"Soon, sweetie. Why don't you have a snack?"

To cut down on the amount and expense of junk food bought from the food carts, they'd eaten a fairly large, early dinner, and there were a variety of snacks packed in the backpack, as well as a refillable water bottle.

"I'm not hungry yet. When will the fireworks start?"

Not soon enough, Meredith thought as she scanned the crowd.

"Hi," she heard Sophie say, and she looked up from the backpack to see Reyna standing at the edge of the quilt.

"Reyna," she said. "You found us. This is my daughter, Sophie. And, Sophie, say hello to Ms. Bishop. We went to school together when I lived here before."

They greeted each other, and Reyna looked at Meredith. "It's unbelievable how much she looks like you. Like a mini version."

"There's definitely no doubt she's mine. Are you here with anybody? There's plenty of room on our quilt."

She made a face. "I'm here on yet another first date, actually. I'm hoping this one doesn't propose during the fireworks finale."

"That bad, huh?"

"You know what they say," an older woman said from behind Meredith, and she turned to see Mrs. Bishop carrying a tote bag with a blanket poking out of the top. "My Reyna is hell on men."

Reyna had mouthed the words *hell on men* as her mother said them, so it was obviously something she'd heard before. "Thanks, Mom."

"Where is this mystery date?" Meredith asked.

"He's getting us caramel apples, because trying to gnaw your way through one of those is totally sexy on a first date."

They laughed and Mrs. Bishop rolled her eyes before heading off to wherever she was spreading her blanket. "There can't be *that* many single men in Blackberry Bay, Reyna. You're going to have to move at some point if you don't find a good one."

"Oh, this one lives twenty minutes away. I figured out a long time ago that the pool in this town is too shallow for me."

"Maybe he's the one?" she asked hopefully.

"I'm trying not to hold the caramel apples against him, so we'll see. I should get back, though, so he doesn't think I ditched him. Let's do lunch or something soon, okay? Sitting down at a table so we can actually catch up and all that."

"Definitely. I'll find out when my mom can hang out with Sophie and let you know."

Reyna said goodbye to Sophie and then, with a wave, headed back to her date. Meredith barely had time to pull out some crackers for Sophie before her parents arrived. She'd been hoping to fill her daughter up some before her dad arrived, since he had a tendency to spoil his granddaughter on the rare occasions they'd gotten together in the past.

Now that they'd be seeing Sophie on a regular

basis, they were going to have to start setting some ground rules. Like maybe no to the giant bag of cotton candy Sophie talked her grandpa into when he took her to swing on the playground for a little while.

Things settled down as the light started to dim. The children were all excited—and hopped up on spun sugar—but everybody was settled on blankets for the most part, with a ring of lawn chairs around the edge of the park for those who couldn't sit on the ground.

"Cam!"

Meredith almost dropped the water bottle she'd been sipping from. And maybe her heart rate picked up and her skin flushed because she'd been startled by her daughter's sudden shout, but maybe not. Following Sophie's gaze, she saw Cam standing on the outskirts of the park, looking around.

And he must have heard Sophie, because he was looking back at her. Sophie was waving desperately to him, but he waited until Meredith sighed and beckoned to him to start walking.

"How come you don't have a blanket?" Sophie demanded when he reached them.

"I didn't know I was supposed to bring one. Mr. and Mrs. Lane, it's good to see you again."

"Neal and Erin will do fine," Meredith's dad said. "And likewise."

"Don't you know how to do fireworks?" Sophie asked, unwilling to let their neighbor's lack of preparation go. "Have you gone to fireworks before?"

He laughed. "Yes, smarty-pants, I've seen fireworks. I've seen them from rooftops and from a boat and some other places, but I've never watched them from a park, so I didn't know the rules."

"We have a big blanket, so you can sit with us," Sophie said, scooching over and patting the empty space next to her.

"The more the merrier," Meredith's mom said. "Do you want some lemonade? Neal bought an entire gallon and some paper cups."

"Because his granddaughter hadn't had nearly enough sugar for one night," Meredith added in a droll tone. And she didn't even bother to help Cam find a graceful way of declining the invitation to share their blanket. With Sophie and Erin both offering, he and Meredith were both doomed.

Cam had no idea how he'd come to be flat on his back on a quilt, next to Meredith. Granted, Sophie was between them, making *ooh* sounds with every colorful burst in the dark sky.

But here he was, once again somehow a part of a family outing with a family that wasn't his. And, despite feeling slightly too old to be lying on the hard ground, he was enjoying himself immensely.

He'd once watched a fireworks display from the bow of a megayacht belonging to one of the richest men in the world. They'd been wearing their finest tuxedos and the crowd of impossibly beautiful women had worn gowns and been draped in stunning jewelry. The liquor had been top-shelf and the actual fireworks display ridiculously ostentatious, to go with the overall theme of the night.

Lying on a quilt in the grass, laughing at the big booms with a little girl and her mom, was so much more enjoyable that he knew, in the future, when he thought of fireworks, he'd think of this night first.

The fourth or fifth time Sophie asked if this burst was the finale, he turned his head sideways to look at Meredith just as she did the same. Their gazes locked over the top of her daughter's head and they smiled together.

She turned back to the fireworks first, and for a moment he watched her profile—the way exploding colors lit up her face.

Then he noticed Erin was watching him watch her daughter and almost gave himself whiplash looking back to the sky. He didn't need Meredith's mother getting any ideas.

He had enough of his own.

Since making the decision to head downtown and join the celebration, he'd been trying to convince himself he was *not* looking for Meredith. She'd mentioned the Fourth of July event in passing and Sophie had brought it up several times, but he hadn't thought much of it until her SUV pulled out of the driveway. Sitting in a quiet cottage with a cat who'd refused to have anything to do with him that day—for reasons only she knew—had filled him with a weird sense of loneliness.

Cam was accustomed to being alone. But he wasn't used to being lonely.

So he'd decided he'd drive downtown and experience a small-town Fourth of July celebration because he had nothing better to do. He wasn't *deliberately* looking for Meredith, but he also hadn't been sorry when he heard the familiar shouting of his name from Sophie.

"Okay, this is probably the finale," he heard Meredith tell her as a long barrage of color and sound started.

Cam let the child's excitement wash over him as he took in the fireworks finale. It was a lot more impressive than he'd anticipated, and he joined in with the rest of the crowd's applause and whistles of appreciation when it was over.

"That was the best ever," Sophie shouted, still clapping her hands.

"Definitely," he agreed. "I've never enjoyed a fireworks show more."

Meredith gave him a skeptical look, but he was

telling the truth so he didn't look away until she stood up. "It's way past bedtime, Sophie, so let's get this picked up and the quilt folded so we can get home eventually."

By the time they'd repacked the backpack and Erin's tote, made a trip to the trash barrel and folded the quilt, there seemed to be a mass exodus out of the park.

"Does everybody in Blackberry Bay come to this park for the Fourth?" he asked, stepping out of the way of a double stroller.

"Pretty much," Neal said. "What else are we going to do?"

That was a good point, since that was why Cam had shown up. What else was he going to do? "There's going to be an actual traffic jam getting out of here."

Meredith shrugged one shoulder. "That's why it's best not to be in a hurry. And since Sophie will probably be out like a light two minutes after the car starts, I'm not worried about it."

With everything picked up, there didn't seem to be anything left for Cam to do. "I guess I'll get going, then. I'm hoping even though I haven't been here long enough to remember street names and land-marks, I'll remember how to get back to my car. I remember I'm near a bookstore."

"I hope you had a good time," Meredith said, and their gazes locked over Sophie's head.

"I did."

"Oh!" Erin's interjection startled them both. "I want to introduce Sophie to my friends over there. We'll probably be a little bit, so why don't you finish up here and we'll just meet you back at your car, Meredith? We saw it in front of the paddleboard shop, so I know where you're parked."

"I'll help you carry stuff," Neal offered, but Erin immediately shook her head.

"You'll come with me so we can show off your granddaughter together. Cam can help Meredith carry stuff to her car."

"Mom." There was a subtle warning in Meredith's voice, but her parents were already walking away, with Sophie skipping between them.

Erin Lane definitely got zero points for subtlety, Cam thought with a chuckle. Meredith didn't look as amused as he was, though. Her face was flushed and she rolled her eyes when he looked at her.

"I can get this stuff to my car by myself, so you're off the hook."

"I'm not going to let you carry all this without help."

"What you and my mother both seem to have forgotten is that I carried all of it from my car to *here* without help, so it stands to reason I can carry it back by myself just fine."

"But now it's dark," he countered because, even without her mother's interference, he wouldn't just walk away and leave Meredith to fend for herself. "You shouldn't be doing it alone."

"I feel like I should apologize for my mom, since she volunteered you for this and now you feel like you have to help, but you really don't have to, you know. There's not as much stuff as it looks like there is and, *again*, I carried it here with no problem."

"What is it you've learned about me so far that makes you think I'm the kind of man who'll just stand here and watch a woman lug a bunch of stuff to her car?"

"Well, you start lawnmowers at seven thirty on a Sunday morning."

"Fair." He picked up the backpack before she could. "But I'm still carrying this."

"Fine. But then you'll be even more lost and you'll never figure out where you parked *your* car."

"It's a small town. I'm bound to find it eventually."

They joined in the crowd leaving the area, and several times they had to pause while somebody spoke to Meredith. She introduced him and said he was staying in the Archambault cottage for the summer, which got him some curious looks. But, for the most part, people wanted to get home and didn't ask questions. Because it was late before the sky was dark enough for fireworks in July, there were a whole lot of kids who were up past their bedtimes.

They made small talk while they walked. She pointed out businesses he might be interested in, and shared some stories from growing up in the town. He was surprised the years of living in San Diego hadn't spoiled her, but she honestly seemed happy to be back in a town that didn't even have a Starbucks.

While he had no intention of admitting it out loud, she was also right. By the time they reached her SUV, he had no idea where he was or where he might be in relation to where he'd parked.

Meredith hit the button for her liftgate and then tossed the quilt into the back, along with the two stuffed animals and the foam flag Sophie had talked her grandfather into buying for her from the street vendors. He waited until she was done and then set the backpack in next to the quilt.

"Thank you," she said as she hit the button to close the liftgate, and they moved out of the way, onto the sidewalk. "Maybe next year I'll remember she always leaves with more than she arrived with, and I'll bring a backpack *and* an empty tote."

"She's worth it, though. I've watched some impressive fireworks displays from some pretty fancy places, but I've never enjoyed them as much as I did tonight."

Meredith's face softened, and the warmth in her eyes made him want to pull her into his arms. "Thank you for saying that."

"It's the truth. Her excitement is infectious, and I like your parents, too." He paused. Took a tentative step that halved the distance between them. "And you. I like spending time with you."

He heard the sharp intake of her breath, but she didn't back away from him. "I should have invited you to come with us."

"So you're not mad I crashed your quilt party?"

She smiled, her gaze fixed on his mouth. "Not at all."

Everything faded away except for her brown eyes and the smell of her hair and his need to touch her. He reached out and ran his fingers down her hand, giving her the chance to pull away without it being a big deal.

But she slid her fingers through his and, as he tugged her closer, she tilted her face up to him.

As he lowered his lips to hers, anticipation sizzled across his skin and he had to concentrate on not hauling her into his arms and kissing her until they couldn't breathe, the way he desperately wanted to.

Instead, he kept his fingers interlocked with hers and with his free hand, cupped the back of her head as his mouth claimed hers. Their breath mingled and she sighed when he ran his tongue over her bottom lip.

He wanted to devour her—to kiss her for hours—but he settled for a taste. Then, with a reluctance she could surely feel, he broke off the kiss and rested his forehead against hers for a few seconds before lifting his head.

Tears shimmered in her eyes, but she chuckled as she did her best to blink them back. "Wow."

"Are you okay?"

She nodded before wiping away the single tear that escaped. "You're the first man I've kissed since I lost my husband. My first *first kiss* since the day I met him."

"I'm sorry. I didn't… I…" He sucked in a breath. "I don't really know what to say right now."

As if realizing she'd just brought her husband into a moment when she should have been totally focused on the kiss they just shared, she winced. "No, I'm sorry. I shouldn't have said that."

He brushed his thumb over her cheek. "I get it. It's a pretty big deal, and I'm honored it was me, I guess."

"You guess?" She laughed with him. "Well, *I guess* I always knew I'd have another first kiss someday. I didn't expect to be kissing my annoying neighbor, though."

"Annoying neighbor?"

"*Really* annoying neighbor, actually."

He refused to be insulted. "Really annoying as in you really don't like me and wish I'd just move away already, or really annoying in that you actually like me a lot, but don't want to?"

Pink spread across her cheeks. "Are those my only two choices?"

That was answer enough for him. Plus, over her shoulder, he could see her family approaching, though it was taking them a while to work through the crowd, since her parents appeared to know everybody in town.

"Fair warning, your parents and Sophie are on their way over here."

Her eyes widened, and then she sucked in a deep breath, obviously trying to calm herself. "Okay. I... No offense, but I'd prefer none of them know my mother's scheme to get us alone actually bore fruit."

"I wouldn't say it bore fruit, exactly."

She arched one eyebrow. "What, *exactly*, do you think my mother was intending to happen if you think kissing me isn't the fruit?"

He could feel the blush creeping over his cheeks and hoped the light was too dim for her to see it.

"Cam!"

"I swear, every time my child says your name, it sounds like she's saying it in all caps, with three exclamation points."

He laughed as he waved at Sophie. "It does, which

is good for my ego. I'm not used to having anybody so excited to see me."

Since he'd chosen that second to look back at Meredith, he caught the pink that colored her cheeks, even in the dim light. So, whether she'd admit it or not, her daughter wasn't the only Price lady who was happy to have him around.

Once they'd gotten Sophie buckled into the back seat with her stuffed animals, Cam shook hands with her parents, trying to ignore the speculative glances Erin kept casting his way.

"Oh, Cam," Meredith said when he started to walk away, and he turned with his heart thumping in his chest. Surely she wouldn't reference the kiss in front of her parents, even if Sophie was closed in the car? "You're going the wrong way."

"What?"

"You mentioned the bookstore before, when you were talking about where you parked. You want to go *that* way and take a left after the post office. Your car should be on that street."

"Thanks," he said, reversing direction. He waved at Sophie as he passed the car, and smiled at Meredith.

She smiled back, her cheeks still pink, which wasn't lost on her mother. Erin gave him a little wink as she passed. Yes, he thought as he walked away, there were definitely ideas being had. All the way around.

Chapter Ten

Meredith watched the numbers slowly ticking away on her bedside clock, wishing she was still asleep because she'd been having a rather interesting dream about Cam that ended at a frustrating time. Premature awakening.

But she was also thankful she was awake because she really didn't need dreams like that making her want things she really shouldn't be wanting. He was a bad idea, and she knew it.

7:54.

She blamed the kiss. Even though she'd been battling her attraction to him from essentially the first moment they met, it was still unexpected. Their first kiss.

And, if she had any sense at all, their last.

Starting about a year after Devin died, she had a few well-meaning friends in California who urged her to get out there and get back on the horse. She was too young to go without sex, they'd said, and she should find somebody to have a fling with, even if it went nowhere.

She hadn't thought she had it in her to have a one-night stand, but when Cam had kissed her last night, she'd realized she did. If she didn't have the responsibility of a daughter to take care of and a dog waiting for them at home—probably anxious despite the meds they gave him before fireworks and thunderstorms—she would have gone with Cam anywhere. Including his bed.

But now, in the clear light of morning, she could see how disastrous that would have been. He lived next door, so there would be no avoiding him. Her daughter adored him. And he was leaving Blackberry Bay at some point, probably right around the time Sophie would start school, so not only would she be alone, but she'd be *totally* alone. The first day with neither Cam nor her daughter was going to feel unbearably empty.

The clock ticked over to eight o'clock, and a

few seconds later, she heard the lawnmower start next door.

Chuckling, Meredith threw back her blanket and got ready to start her day. It was a day that was going to include some housekeeping, a playdate for Sophie with two girls whose family had rented the house two docks down for the summer and a trip to the market for her. What it was *not* going to include was spying on her neighbor while he did yardwork, hoping he took his shirt off again.

Hours later, Oscar absolutely lost his mind when somebody knocked on the slider just as Meredith finished preparing dinner. The barking was so sudden and intense her heart thumped in her chest and Sophie put her hands over her ears.

Cam was standing on the other side of the glass, making a face that clearly said "I'm so sorry."

She hadn't seen him since he kissed her and for a moment all she could do was stare at him, remembering the incredible hunger for him she'd been denying until his mouth touched hers. She'd been trying so hard not to think about that.

Then she told Oscar to hush—not that he listened—and waved for Cam to come in, but Sophie had already left her chair and was rushing to open the slider for him.

"That's quite an alarm system you have," he said,

ruffling her hair. Then he looked at Meredith, their gazes locking. "Sorry about the chaos."

"At least you feel bad about it. Elinor does it on purpose, several times a day."

"I did speak to her about it, but you know... She's a cat." He smiled and she had to make a deliberate effort not to stare at his mouth.

"So, what's up? And be honest. You smelled the lasagna come out of the oven, didn't you?"

"Lasagna?" His eyes lit up, and Meredith pulled another plate out of the cabinet. "You know it's summer, right?"

"It's an easy dish to make too much of, so you can freeze the leftovers. Then you just heat some up when you're not in the mood to cook, you know?"

"So what you're saying is that you have too much."

She laughed and gestured to the table. "Have a seat. Sophie, take this plate and then get Cam some silverware and a drink, please."

"I feel bad about crashing your dinner, especially after crashing your quilt party last night," he said, but he was taking a seat at the table when he said it.

Sophie did as she was asked, including pouring a glass of iced tea for Cam without spilling a drop. The entire time, Meredith tried not to get emotionally stuck in the realization of how good it felt to watch Sophie chattering away to somebody other than her about the playdate she'd had earlier, and how good he was at asking the right questions to keep her talking.

When Cam went back to New York City at the end of the summer, Sophie was going to be devastated.

That thought almost killed her appetite as she cut and plated three servings of lasagna. She'd spent a lot of time thinking about how *she* would feel if she got into a relationship with Cam and then he left. But she hadn't considered just how attached her daughter already was to the man.

Sophie had made so much progress on coming out of her shell since they'd arrived in town—the shell she'd withdrawn into when she lost her father. Would losing another man she cared about, even if she'd known him for only a couple of months, set her back?

As they ate, she couldn't stop dwelling on it, but it was fairly obvious she was too late when it came to keeping Sophie from growing attached to Cam. She couldn't get enough of his attention, and he honestly didn't seem to mind. He listened to her and laughed with her, and occasionally he'd make eye contact with Meredith and smile. It wasn't really possible for them to have a conversation, but he seemed content to eat lasagna and listen to her daughter. She'd moved on to describing the weird bug she'd found under a rock.

"I don't know," Cam was saying. "Maybe you

should get a book about bugs the next time you go to the library."

Meredith groaned. "If she develops some kind of passion for bugs and starts collecting them, she's keeping them in *your* house. Fair warning."

"I don't think Elinor would like that," Sophie said, her expression serious all of a sudden. "They would probably scare her. Or maybe she'd try to eat them and get sick."

"I don't think Elinor's afraid of anything," Cam said.

"And she's a very grown-up cat," Meredith added. "I don't think she'd try to eat the bugs. But just to be safe, let's leave any bugs in the garden where we find them."

Once they were finished eating, Meredith refused his offer to help clean up. "I like to listen to an audiobook while I clean up and load the dishwasher, and I'm almost to the end of the mystery I'm listening to. You're coming between me and the answer to whodunit."

He laughed and held up his hands. "I'll let you get back to your book, then. Can you, uh, step outside for a second?"

Her heart hammered in her chest, and she looked at Sophie, who was drawing a picture of a bug on the grocery list they kept on the fridge—presumably her way of remembering to look for insect books at the library since she was a precocious reader but didn't have the patience for writing words.

"For a second, I guess," she said.

She was *not* going to kiss him again. Especially in her backyard, where Sophie could see her. That wasn't a conversation she wanted to have with her daughter anytime soon. But especially now, when she couldn't even explain this attraction to herself.

Once they'd stepped out onto the deck and she'd closed the slider, he cleared his throat. His lack of certainty made her nervous, and she was afraid he was going to launch into an awkward speech about how kissing her had been a huge mistake.

And maybe it was. But she didn't want *him* to think so.

"I actually came over because I have a favor to ask, not to crash your dinner, but after I..." He let the words die away when he realized Sophie might still be within earshot because the windows were open. "After the fireworks, if you know what I mean."

"Fireworks, huh? You're pretty confident in your abilities." When he began stammering, obviously trying to explain himself without Sophie finding out he'd kissed her mom, she laughed and let him off the hook. "I know what you're trying to say, Cam. What's the favor?"

"It's a big one."

The seriousness in his expression made her realize

what he wanted to ask her before he said the words, and her stomach knotted. So much for slowly pulling Sophie back from their neighbor. "Did you finally come to your senses about needing help with Carolina's belongings?"

"Yeah, it's pretty overwhelming. I had to talk to her lawyer about some paperwork yesterday and he suggested I reach out to the church ladies or some of Carolina's friends to help me out, but I don't feel ready to do that."

"That's a lot of people rummaging around in your personal business."

"Exactly. I just don't want to talk about it that much. And you already know, so I don't have to keep telling the story over and over."

She definitely understood that, having had to explain about Devin's passing over and over. "On the flip side, you'd have a lot of people around you who actually knew Carolina. And your father. Have you considered that?"

He nodded. "I thought about it. And once I have everything in order, I can reach out to see who wants any of it and maybe have a few conversations. Ask some questions. And she talks about a friend in her journals a lot—Tess Weaver, who I think you mentioned—and I do want to talk to her at some point. But having them in my house for days means I can't really avoid them if it's too hard or I just need a break from thinking about it all."

"I wish I knew Tess better and that I remembered your grandmother or father more. But we lived on the other side of the bay, in the neighborhood that didn't have lakefront price tags. And you know how kids are. We knew almost everybody, but we didn't pay attention to people."

"I don't know if Tess knows who I am," he said quietly. "Carolina's journals are jumbled up, so I'm getting little bits of her life in random order."

"I have no idea if she knows for sure, but she must suspect. She had to know Carolina had a grandson and here you are, the right age and a total stranger to Blackberry Bay, showing up to take care of her cottage and her cat. Have you asked the lawyer if Tess has asked questions?"

"No, but he doesn't strike me as the kind of guy to gossip, and he mentioned he's not originally from here, so people might not be as comfortable pressuring him for answers." He blew out a breath and ran a hand over his hair. "It's just a lot, you know?"

There was no way she'd be able to tell him no. She'd made the offer, after all. And she couldn't ignore the fact he was going through an extraordinarily tough time in his life and he didn't have anybody else to help him. He was alone in Blackberry Bay, trying to take a cottage full of random pieces and figure out the puzzle that was his biological father's life.

"Sophie and I would be happy to help," she said, because there was nothing else she could say.

Of course she'd have Sophie with her, since she was still too young for Meredith to leave her in their house alone for more than a few minutes, even if she was next door, but her presence would also have the added benefit of making sure Meredith and Cam weren't alone behind closed doors.

Except when Sophie inevitably curled up on his deck with a book or played with Oscar in the backyard.

"When do you want us to get started?" she asked. "And is there a time of day that's better for you, work-wise?"

"I have to go back to the city for a meeting I have to be present for. I'm planning to leave very early Tuesday morning, and it'll probably be just one overnight, but it might be two if there's something really pressing." His jaw clenched, tension tightening the lines of his face. "But no more than that."

"What about Elinor?"

He cursed under his breath. "I hadn't thought about it. And don't look at me like that. I'm not used to having another living being to worry about, but I would have remembered her. I wouldn't have just left. But I'm afraid if I ask the shelter to board her for a couple of days, she'll be upset. The last time she was there, Carolina never came back."

It was sweet that he was considering Elinor's feelings, since he was still denying she was actually his cat. "We can take care of her, and Sophie found the spare key to your cottage under a painted rock last week. I meant to tell you that, by the way. Elinor pretty much does her own thing anyway, but we'll make sure she has food and water. And you know Sophie will sit in the hammock with her if she's feeling lonely."

"I appreciate that. I'll do my best to keep it to one overnight." He sighed. "My parents will come at me hard, not wanting me to leave again, but I'm not done here."

But he would be, eventually. And that was something Meredith couldn't let herself forget.

It was dark by the time Cam finally saw the "welcome to Blackberry Bay" sign reflected in his headlights. He had a nagging headache, he was out of road snacks and he'd gotten his first speeding ticket an hour ago.

The officer had asked him where he was going in such a hurry and he'd confessed he had no excuse because he didn't want to admit the truth out loud. *I'm trying to get back before Sophie goes to bed.*

Around the time he'd hit the New Hampshire border, the thoughts of business he'd been turning over and over in his mind had given way to the awareness he'd be seeing Meredith soon. The trip to New York City hadn't gone well—a man they'd trusted to run a development company they'd acquired several years back had been embezzling money from them and it was going to be ugly—but thinking about what was waiting for him in Blackberry Bay definitely lowered his blood pressure.

The way Meredith smiled at him. The excitement in Sophie's voice when she saw him. The hammock next to the water, where he could close his eyes and let go—for a few minutes—of the stress that came with being cast in the role of heir to the Maguire business holdings. And a cat who, every once in a while, deigned to allow him to stroke her hair.

Sophie would definitely be in bed by now, but Meredith would still be up. Maybe she'd see his car pull in and step outside to ask him how his trip had gone. He didn't particularly care to talk about the trip, but he wanted to hear her voice.

His phone rang and his mother's number lit up on the car's info screen, scattering the good thoughts he'd managed to gather like leaves in an autumn wind. His thumb hovered over the red decline button on the wheel, but he'd rather deal with her now and be done with it than have her keep calling once he was home.

No, not *home*. The cottage.

He accepted the call. "Hello, Mom."

"I'm going to stop by after this ridiculous wedding shower is over. We need to talk."

"I won't be there. I told you I was leaving after my final meeting with Dad."

Her annoyed sigh echoed through the car's speakers. "I asked you to extend your stay in the city."

"And I told you I wasn't going to do that." Of course she hadn't considered that, when he said no to her demand disguised as a request, he'd meant it. His mother got what she wanted by ignoring that two-letter word. "But I'm driving right now. Go ahead and talk."

"No, I'm not going to talk about this over the phone." She sounded more agitated than usual. "And I told you I'm at a function."

Talk about *this* over the phone. Talk about what?

For a moment, he thought she knew where he was. That she knew he was, at that very moment, navigating the main street of Blackberry Bay on his way back to his biological grandmother's cottage. That the secret she'd been keeping for his entire life was out.

But that was ridiculous. He'd been careful not to give any indication that a letter had arrived to wreak havoc on his life. And he'd always been careful about privacy settings and location beacons, so unless his mother had a side gig with an intelligence agency, she shouldn't know where he was.

"I'll let you know when I'm going to be back in the city and we can talk about whatever it is then," he said, not bothering to tell her it would be a while.

"I hope you'll have whatever this is out of your system by then."

He inhaled deeply through the nose and blew the breath out even more slowly through his mouth. Pushing back would only extend the conversation and he was almost back to the cottage. He wanted this to be over before he turned onto the small, quiet road that followed the shore of the bay.

"I'll be in touch when I'm planning to return," he said, not addressing her suggestion he was just going through some kind of early midlife crisis.

She had to have the last word on when he was returning—as soon as possible—and give him another reminder that he was inconveniencing his father, so he wasn't able to disconnect the call until he was pulling into his driveway.

He did his best to shove New York City out of his head again, but it was a lot harder to do with his mother's voice still echoing around in his mind. After grabbing his overnight bag from the back seat, he let himself into the cottage and took a deep breath.

It still smelled strongly of a woman he didn't know, but it brought him comfort. He could almost imagine Carolina wrapping her arms around him and giving him a long, tight hug.

"Well, that's ridiculous," he muttered as Elinor appeared to greet him. She rubbed against his legs, leaving what looked like a quarter of her fur on his suit pants, but when he bent down to pet her, she got snippy and walked away.

He probably deserved that. "Hey, at least I didn't board you at the shelter or someplace while I was gone. I let you stay in your home, with Meredith and Sophie taking care of you."

She had no interest in listening to what he had to say.

Still agitated, Cam dropped his bag next to the sofa and walked straight through the cottage to the back slider. Maybe looking out over the water would soothe his nerves and help him refocus on the man he'd somehow become since arriving here.

A man with a cat. A man with a fun, sexy neighbor. A man who liked to play catch with Sophie and her yapping little dog. He was a man who sat on quilts in the grass and ate cotton candy. He had a library card.

He liked this version of himself.

Chapter Eleven

Meredith caught a glimpse of Cam standing on his back deck and froze as her pulse quickened and she felt that thrill she wanted so badly to deny, but that grew stronger every time she saw him.

He looked different tonight. The suit, of course. And even though she'd spent years around men who practically lived in business suits, the sight of Cam in his took her breath away. The man *really* knew how to wear a suit.

But it wasn't just the clothing. There was a rigidity to his bearing that she could see from her window. As if every single muscle in his body was so tense he would break if he tried to bend.

Things obviously hadn't gone well in the city and she couldn't bear to see him so unhappy. So alone.

Sophie was already asleep, with Oscar tucked in beside her, so Meredith threw a loose sweatshirt over her tank top and shorts and slid her feet into sandals. Slowly and quietly, so as not to disturb Oscar and get him going, she slipped out through the sliding door and closed it behind her.

She was halfway across her yard when her movement caught his attention, and he raised one eyebrow as she approached, but didn't smile.

"Welcome back," she said when she was close enough to be heard without raising her voice.

"It's good to be back."

She reached his side and turned to look over the bay, as he'd been doing. The water was an inky blackness reflecting the moon and the lights of the town. "You don't look very happy about it, to be honest."

"I *am* happy to be back. I'm just having a little trouble shaking off some earlier unpleasantness."

"I take it you were right about your parents trying to keep you from returning."

He snorted. "That's an understatement."

"It can't be easy for them. The reason you're here, I mean."

His jaw clenched for a few seconds and she realized she'd hit a hot button. "They don't actually know why I'm here. I told them I've never taken a vacation and I was spending the summer on a lake and would work remotely. That's all they needed to know."

She suspected there was more to it than that, but she didn't press. "I'm sorry they can't respect that."

"To top it all off, Elinor is ignoring me. She came to the door and then rubbed against my leg. But when I went to pet her, she twitched her tail at me and walked away. Before I came out here, she was very deliberately sitting with her back to me."

Meredith chuckled. "Of course she was. She's glad you're back, but she's still going to punish you for being away."

"She *is* a woman, after all."

"Oh, you're funny," she said, but he barely managed a smile despite his attempt at humor. "Don't take this the wrong way, but you look like a man who could really use a hug."

He looked startled, and then thoughtfulness settled over his face. "I had a nanny who used to hug me a lot. She was with me until it was time to go off to boarding school."

"How long has it been since you've *had* a hug?"

"A real hug and not one of those polite social hugs? I'm not sure. I guess I went off to boarding school for sixth grade, so it's been a while. My family's not big on physical contact."

She was *not* going to cry for this man. Families

showed affection in many different ways, and not being a hugger was far from unusual. He was a man who'd obviously been raised in a world of privilege and financial security, so she couldn't weep for him.

But she could hug him.

Meredith opened her arms as she closed the distance between them, and she saw his recognition of her intent in the widening of his eyes. When she'd wrapped her arms around him and rested her face against his chest, she realized he was holding his breath.

She squeezed a little, and then smiled when his arms wrapped around her shoulders. His chest rose and fell as it should, but she could feel his heartbeat and it was beating almost as fast as hers.

His muscles slowly relaxed, but she kept holding him until he exhaled slowly and rested his cheek against her hair.

"Hugging is nice," he said so quietly it was almost a whisper.

"Yes, it is. And hugs are important, too. Humans need hugs sometimes."

"Kissing is also nice."

She laughed, the sound partially muffled by his suit coat. "So are cupcakes, but you don't have any of those, either."

"If you had to choose between kissing or cupcakes, which would you choose?"

"I guess it would depend on who I'm kissing. And also what kind of cupcake." She lifted her head. "Why? Do you have cupcakes?"

"No, I don't. And let's say it was me you were kissing."

She made a *hmm* sound, just to let him know she had to think about it. "I guess if I had to choose between kissing you or cupcakes that don't exist, I'd choose kissing."

"Good to know. And I'll just point out there are currently no cupcakes, so…"

She couldn't resist this playful, funny side of him, and when she tipped her head farther back so she could see his face, his eyes crinkled with humor. Rolling onto the balls of her feet, she lifted her mouth to his.

His arms tightened around her as their lips met, gently at first, but then with the hunger that the days since their first kiss had built up inside. His hand moved to cup the back of her neck, and she parted her lips as his tongue flicked over them.

She didn't know how long they kissed. Until she ached with wanting him and they were both breathless. Until she was tempted to sneak him into her bedroom and very quietly put an end to the wanting.

And until Elinor stretched up and dug her claws into Cam's lower thigh. "Ow. Cat, that really hurts."

"I think she's jealous," Meredith said, backing

away from him as he bent down to disengage her claws from his pants. It looked like a very expensive suit, too.

"Of course she chooses *now* to decide to speak to me again," he muttered. And then he shook his head when Elinor changed her mind and went back through the cat door.

"I should go back inside, anyway."

He straightened, frowning. "Do you have to? We could sit out here for a little while."

"Sophie's sleeping and I don't know if I'd hear her if she called for me."

"Don't you have one of those monitor things?"

She laughed, shaking her head. "She's six. When we decluttered before moving here, we decided it was time to let that go."

The compulsion to push was clear on his face, but to his credit, he didn't. "I wouldn't want her to wake up in the house alone, so yeah."

She could invite him into *her* house, but somehow she felt that would mean something she wasn't ready for. Not that he'd be climbing into her bed or anything, but after the kiss they'd just shared, it would definitely imply a sort of intimacy.

This wasn't a man she was supposed to be rediscovering intimacy with. She wasn't even sure she was ready for more, and how awkward would it be to have to turn him away and then face him again? Especially since Sophie seemed to consider their back-yards as one these days.

With the taste of him still on her lips, she forced them into a smile. "I really should get back inside. Let me know when you're ready to start sorting stuff in there."

Some of the sparkle went out of his eyes, but he nodded. "I will. And thanks for the hug."

She knew he watched her walking away, but she tried not to feel too self-conscious. And when she reached her deck and glanced back, he lifted his hand in a wave before going inside.

After locking up and turning out the lights, Meredith flopped on her bed with a sigh. Kissing Cam a second time had done nothing to dampen the desire she felt every time she looked at him. If anything, it was going to be even worse.

She should have chosen the imaginary cupcakes.

Cam rubbed the back of his neck, which was stiff from looking down at the legal pad he'd covered with scribbled notes and calculations. Next to it sat reports from several real estate agents he'd spoken to about the property.

Carolina had taken a great deal of pride in her house being one of the only old, authentic lake cottages left on the bay, and the only one on this side of it. She'd stood fast while the others were all replaced with newer summer homes, even as her property taxes rose and took money away from maintaining it.

He appreciated that about her. He really did. But she'd left him in a fairly untenable position when it came to selling it because it needed very badly to be remodeled. It was dated and shabby and her eclectic style wasn't going to appeal to the average buyer. Selling it as it stood would mean selling it for far less than its location merited.

He'd take a beating on the property because a prospective buyer would no doubt hold the cost of bulldozing the place against the sale price. Or, on the off chance they wanted to keep the cottage, they'd definitely want to deduct the cost of remodeling, which would be so substantial he couldn't even wrap his head around it. But because of its location, the hard reality was that somebody—probably a local somebody—who loved the cottage the way it was most likely couldn't afford it.

As far as he could tell, Meredith had been right and his best bet was to empty the cottage and dismantle it. He could shop around and control the demolition costs. Then do some minor improvements to the dock and driveway, before selling it off as a rare waterfront building site on Blackberry Bay.

It was all making his head hurt. He was a man who lived his life for the bottom line. Profits and losses. At the end of the day, those numbers were what mattered to the Maguire family.

But there was no denying the ache in his chest when he imagined watching this cottage being demolished. Underneath its questionable real estate value was a worth Cam didn't have the life skills to calculate. Emotions had no place in business, but he couldn't keep them buried inside anymore.

Too agitated to look at the numbers, he stood and stretched his back, rolling his head slowly to loosen up his neck. Then he made himself a cup of coffee and went out to the deck to drink it and maybe catch a glimpse of Elinor. She'd gone outside earlier, and he didn't think she'd gone back inside again.

It was quiet next door. He knew they were home because Meredith's SUV was still parked in the driveway, but he didn't see Sophie or Oscar in the backyard. They'd screwed some kind of anchor to the deck and attached a long cable, so the dog could have the run of most of the yard without being on a leash, but he was getting better at boundaries and listening, so quite often he was allowed to run free as long as he stayed with Sophie or Meredith.

He hadn't seen Meredith since she went back inside last night, after he kissed her. He'd thought about almost nothing except that kiss—and how much he wanted to do it again—since she'd walked away, to the point he'd actually pulled out the market analyses on the cottage to distract himself.

Knowing it was a mistake to get involved with her and being able to stop himself were two different things, and he was failing miserably at the latter. While part of his brain was aware that a widow putting down roots in Blackberry Bay and her little girl had no place in his life, that logical voice was easy to ignore, like a boring teacher lecturing in a classroom.

Then she stepped out onto her deck and his breath caught in his throat. Her dark blond hair was gathered into a messy knot on top of her head, showing off her neck, and she was laughing at something. Probably something Sophie said, since her daughter was right behind her.

He could keep the cottage, that irresponsible voice in his head said. A lot of people in the Maguire circle had summer homes they visited on weekends, or occasionally even for an entire week. He didn't have to let it go.

Meredith turned, her gaze locking with his. He hadn't moved or made a noise that would have gotten her attention, so she was looking for him. He smiled and, after a few seconds, she smiled back. But Sophie was tugging at her hand, trying to drag her to the flower garden they were in the process of expanding, and the eye contact was lost.

She didn't wave him over and Sophie hadn't seen

him, so he stayed where he was and enjoyed the happy sounds of them playing in the garden. Oscar played around them, occasionally trying to roll in the loose dirt, and Elinor even appeared from wherever she'd been to sit on the deck rail and watch.

After twenty minutes or so, Meredith stood and brushed dirt off her navy shorts. He watched her say something to Sophie, and then the little girl ran across the yard, straight toward him.

"Cam!" She ran up the steps and stopped in front of him. Oscar stopped short at the bottom of the steps when Elinor jumped off the rail to sit at the top. She couldn't do anything about the people, but she didn't like the dog on her deck.

"Hey, Sophie. How's the gardening going?"

"Oscar peed on the daisies."

He chuckled. "At least he didn't eat them, I guess."

"Ew. Mommy wants to know when we're going to help you clean your house up."

"Since you're helping me, whenever is best for you. I do most of my work in the morning, so maybe in the afternoons? But I can work around her schedule."

"Okay, hold on." She took off running again before he could stop her, and he watched her tell Meredith what he'd said—or probably some approximation of it, complete with hands waving and bouncing on her toes.

Then she raced back. "Mommy said we'll come over tomorrow after lunch."

"Sounds good. Tell your mommy I said thank you."

"Okay. We're going to the market after we wash up. Do you want to go?"

He did need a couple of things and a trip to the store would be a lot more fun if he went with them, but he recognized using Sophie as a messenger was a pretty strong indicator Meredith wanted a little space from him today. Whether she was having second thoughts about kissing him or she was struggling with *wanting* to kiss him, she was staying in her own yard today. If he told Sophie he wanted to go, he knew Meredith would eventually be forced to give in, and he'd already made that mistake once.

"I have stuff to do so I can't go today," he said, "but I hope you have fun."

He smiled as he watched her run back to her mother again. As far as he could tell, Sophie had two speeds—sitting still with a book or on the run—and he wished he could muster a fraction of her energy.

Maybe he would if he slept at night instead of tossing and turning, thinking about kissing his neighbor.

As if she somehow sensed he was thinking about her, Meredith paused on her way inside and looked at him. She smiled again, this one a little more genuine, and then waved before disappearing from view.

At least that was something. And she'd be in his house tomorrow, helping him with Carolina's many boxes. As long as he stayed out of her way and respected the distance she'd put between them, they'd be okay.

Whether she'd work her away around to kissing him again, he didn't know. But he certainly hoped so.

Chapter Twelve

"What do you think this is?"

Meredith looked up from the table, where she was sorting boxes of papers, to see Cam holding up a small wooden drying rack. He kept folding it and unfolding it so it looked as if he was playing the skeleton of an accordion.

"It's for drying things. You set it up and then drape things over the wooden dowels to air-dry."

"Oh. Do you want it?"

"No, and stop trying to deal with all the stuff in this house by moving it into my house." She pointed at him. "Yes, I'm onto you. Put that in the donation pile and get back to work."

He laughed and, after adding the drying rack to the corner they'd designated for donations, he disappeared back into the bedroom. She didn't envy him that task since it seemed like Carolina managed to fit more stuff *under* her bed than Meredith even owned, but her own job wasn't much more manageable. The woman had never thrown a piece of paper away, it seemed, and she didn't sort anything by how important it was. The septic redesign documents weren't with the deed. They were "filed" in a box with grocery store receipts from 1982.

"Okay, but what about this?"

Meredith frowned at the metal contraption in his hand. "I think it's for peeling apples, though I can't imagine why it's in the bedroom. And you're supposed to be working in there."

"Despite what I've been led to believe my entire life, it's actually not necessary to work twenty hours a day, seven days a week, to run a business, especially when you employ hundreds of people. I'd rather help. And I bet Sophie likes apples."

"No, Cam." She laughed when he tossed it in the donation pile and walked back into the bedroom.

It was no wonder Sophie had gotten bored with them and gone out to the hammock with her books and her dog an hour before. Oscar was curled up by her side, while Elinor watched them from the sunny deck rail.

It had been a week since Cam had returned from New York City. A week since the kiss on the back deck, which she couldn't stop thinking about during quiet moments. Especially quiet moments at night when she should be sleeping. But during the day, they'd fallen into a rhythm that apparently included pretending it hadn't happened. The pretense was obviously for the best, but it didn't make it any easier. Especially when she'd been in his home every day since for at least a couple of hours in the afternoon, if not more.

When her phone chimed, Meredith had to rummage through the pile of papers to find it. Almost all of it could be tossed, but she'd found a few documents—like the receipt for a new roof a decade ago—that should be kept so they could be noted for the real estate agent and new owner.

Before she could lose herself in her feelings about the fact she'd have new neighbors at some point, and probably before the end of the year if they were year-round residents, she found her phone.

The text message was from Reyna, and as soon as Meredith saw the screen, she was thankful Cam was across the room and in her line of vision. Not only because it was no hardship to watch him work, but because she didn't have to worry about him being behind her and reading her text messages over her shoulder.

You need to find a sitter ASAP so we can do lunch or dinner. Mom got a summer cold, so I've been doing double duty at the bakery and the garage, but I want to hear all about you kissing a hot guy on the side of the road after the fireworks.

Meredith sighed and rested her forehead on her palm. How had she forgotten just how fast gossip spread in Blackberry Bay?

We weren't on the side of the road. We were standing on the sidewalk.

The sidewalk is on the side of the road. That's why it's called a sidewalk.

That made her laugh, despite her dread at having everybody in town dissecting her kiss with Cam. Thank goodness nobody had seen them on his back deck. Smart-ass. I'll check with my mom and get back to you. But we're not talking about the kiss.

Never mind, then.

She blinked, staring at the phone in her hand. Reyna seriously didn't want to have lunch with her if she wasn't willing to spill the details about Cam?

Just kidding. Let me know.

She'd forgotten Reyna had a wicked sense of humor, with a sarcastic bent that had often gone over Meredith's head. Clearly *that* hadn't changed.

"Looks like quite a conversation," Cam said, and Meredith almost dropped her phone. She'd forgotten for a moment that she wasn't alone. "First the face-palm, then laughing and now eye-rolling."

"Oh, it's Reyna. I don't think you met her on the Fourth, but we went to school together. We're picking up our friendship again and trying to come up with a plan to get together."

"You're not going to abandon me in my time of need, are you?"

She laughed. "No, I'm not going to run off and leave you with this mess. Honestly, you've made so many piles, I'm not sure I can even get out."

"I think I'm going to have to rent a truck." He frowned as he looked around the room. "And I need that truck to include a moving crew."

"I saw an ad on the place mat at the café for some guys who haul stuff away. You could probably hire them to load everything up and drop it off…wherever it's going. I know the church said they were happy to have stuff for their rummage sale, but I don't know if they have room to store this much stuff. Have you considered a yard sale?"

"I have not."

"You might want to." When he groaned and returned to the bedroom, Meredith shook her head and went back to her task. While it didn't look like it, they *were* making some headway, and if they had a sale and could get rid of a lot of the clutter, they could get through the process much faster.

Four nights later, Meredith's shoulders ached from being hunched over the table and she'd suffered more than a few paper cuts. It was time for a break, and packing her daughter off to spend the night with her grandmother and then meeting Reyna for dinner was just the break she needed. They met at a place called The Dock, and sat outside, where they could eat dinner and have a couple of drinks while overlooking the bay.

"So let's catch up." Reyna grinned and propped her chin on her hands once they'd ordered. "But let's focus on what's been going on in your life since the Fourth of July."

Meredith tried to laugh off the insinuation there was something to tell, but she could feel the telltale blush across her cheeks. "There's nothing to tell. It was a kiss."

Actually two kisses, but Reyna didn't know about the second and she had no intention of telling her. Of telling *anybody*, no matter how disappointed her friend looked.

"Oh, how did *your* Fourth of July first date go?"

Meredith asked, hoping to deflect the conversation away from herself. "The caramel apple guy."

"Honestly? Not bad. I mean, sure, the caramel apples were awkward, but I guess it's like my mom said—do you really want to spend the rest of your life with a man you can't eat a caramel apple in front of?"

"She does make a good point."

"He's funny and smart and there was no sign of a proposal or future in-laws hiding in the bushes waiting to meet me, so I agreed to a second date."

"And it's not to his house to have Sunday dinner with his mom?"

Reyna laughed and shook her head. "Nope, we're going to a restaurant in Concord that some friends recommended. Neutral grounds—but a more private setting than sitting on a blanket in the middle of the entire population of Blackberry Bay."

A man stopped next to their table, catching Meredith's attention, and when she looked up, it took her only a few seconds to place him. The thick, almost black hair and bright blue eyes. Dimples. That little bit of scruff that kept him from being too pretty. Brady Nash had been the indisputable hottest boy in Blackberry Bay.

She caught Reyna's eye-roll, but she stood to give him a quick hug. "Brady, you haven't changed at all. How have you been?"

"Good, same as always. I heard you were back, but this is the first time I've seen you." The dimples faded as he looked at Reyna, who hadn't stood up. "Hi, Reyna."

"Hey."

"I'll let you get back to your dinner," he said when it became awkwardly obvious Reyna had nothing else to say. "It was good to see you, Meredith. I'm sure we'll run into each other now and then."

Once she was seated and they were alone, Meredith leaned close. "What was that about?"

"What?" When Meredith only arched her eyebrow, Reyna sighed. "Brady? Whatever."

"Whatever? That's all you're going to give me?"

"You tell me yours and I'll tell you mine."

"Fair." She was cornered and there really wasn't *that* much to tell, so she told it. All of it. From meeting Cam to their second kiss and how nothing had happened since.

"And *why* has nothing happened since?" Reyna asked.

"I don't know. There's Sophie, of course. And he'll be leaving, you know. What is the point of a relationship that has an expiration date?"

"I'd make the argument you're already in a relationship. But now that you mention him leaving, why is he here at all? Especially in Carolina's cottage? I've heard he was a relation of some sort, but he didn't have to stay here to settle her estate."

Meredith was reminded with a start that not *everybody* in Blackberry Bay knew Cam was Michael Archambault's son. Certainly some did, but this seemed to be one of the rare instances in which they all kept their mouths shut. And it wasn't Meredith's secret to divulge.

"If you have to settle an estate, why not spend the summer on the shore of the bay while you do it?" She took a sip of her drink and then leaned back in her chair. "Okay, now you. Why don't you like Brady?"

"I don't dislike him. I just don't..." Reyna shook her head. "He has a reputation, you know. Everybody in Blackberry Bay thinks he's the most charming ladies' man to ever grace the planet."

"That's not a surprise. They always thought that."

"We went out once."

Meredith let that sink in. Reyna and Brady? Reyna was gorgeous, of course, but she and Brady were so different, and Reyna had never gone for the popular boys. "I take it didn't go well?"

"Let's just say that his title as a ladies' man is not merited, unless he's dating a lot of women who only have five minutes to spare," Reyna said, and then she took a long drink. "And that includes the time it took to get our pants off."

As her meaning sank in, Meredith had to put her

napkin to her mouth to muffle the laughter. Reyna nodded and they laughed together for so long, other diners started giving them stern side-eyes.

"Poor Brady," Meredith said when she could finally speak again.

"Poor Brady? Trust me. It was poor *me* that night."

By the time they left the restaurant, Meredith's stomach ached from laughing, but she felt younger and lighter than she had in a very long time. She'd have to talk to her mom and see if she'd be willing to make a sleepover with her granddaughter a monthly thing. Somehow Meredith didn't think she'd mind.

Reyna lived within walking distance and didn't want a ride, so they parted ways at Meredith's SUV, but not before she circled back to their earlier conversation. "So, if Sophie's spending the night with your mom, you'll be all alone tonight."

"Yes, and they took Oscar with them and won't be back until after lunch, so I'm planning to sleep in tomorrow." She was almost as excited about not having to get out of bed as she'd been about a night out.

"You're missing the point."

"What point? Yes, I'll be alone tonight."

"But you don't have to be." Reyna grinned. "*That* is my point."

Meredith's skin heated. She hadn't been missing that point. She'd been trying to ignore it. "And then what happens tomorrow? I can't avoid him after because he lives next door and my daughter spends half her time in his yard because I haven't bought a hammock yet. And honestly, even if I do buy one, she'll still be in his yard because she likes him and—"

"Stop." Reyna actually looked annoyed with her. "You managed in two sentences to take a conversation about you scratching an itch that hasn't been scratched in a long time and make it about your kid. And yeah, I know she's the center of your world, but you also need to take care of you. It's called self-care."

Meredith sighed. "Trust me, I'm familiar with self-care, if you know what I mean."

Reyna laughed, and then covered her mouth. "I'm sorry. I shouldn't laugh but—"

"I laugh, because what else are you going to do?"

"You can stop worrying about tomorrow and definitely stop worrying about him leaving at the end of the summer. It's okay to just have a little fun, Meredith."

She didn't want to stand on the sidewalk arguing about whether or not she should sleep with her neighbor, so she nodded. "I'll think about it."

"No. *Stop* thinking about it. Just do it." When Meredith opened her mouth to explain she wasn't sure she could do that, Reyna groaned. "Go home, shave your legs and then go ask the sexy neighbor if you can borrow a cup of sugar."

Cam heard the car door close and waited, but he didn't hear a second door. He knew Sophie was spending the night at her grandparents' house, of course. She'd talked about nothing but her sleepover all morning. But that hadn't meant Meredith would be alone. She could have friends over or…

Sighing, he closed the book he'd been reading and tossed it aside. He didn't want to think about the *or*. If he had to bet, he'd put money against her bringing some guy home, but anything was possible. She was single. She could do as she pleased.

But now that he knew she was alone, he couldn't stop thinking about that fact. As much as he liked the little kid, having Sophie around all the time wasn't exactly conducive to romance, and she wouldn't be back until tomorrow.

Try as he might, he couldn't come up with a reasonable excuse for knocking on her door and starting a conversation. What possible reason could he have for going over there? Borrowing a cup of sugar?

When he realized he was doing nothing but sitting around waiting, he decided to get up and do something. He'd start with taking the box of gardening tools he'd inexplicably found scattered around the house out to the shed. Why Carolina had a gardening shed full of all manner of junk and kept her gardening tools in the kitchen and bathroom was beyond him, but putting things where they belonged could only help the process in the long run.

While he was out there, he poked around a bit, and found out his grandmother had had a fondness for metal yard things. Doodads. Whatever one called the decorative things that walked a fine line between art and recycling pile.

A box of wind chimes caught his eye and he pulled them out. One set was made to look like a bunch of metal hummingbirds, while three of them were just whimsical shapes in brightly colored metal. There were metal hangers for them that were meant to be driven into the ground, rather than hanging the chimes from above.

He didn't remember ever hearing a wind chime in real life. And since he had nothing better to do, since it appeared Meredith wasn't going to take advantage of her child-free night by visiting her neighbor, he set the box out on the lawn and closed up the shed.

Then he pushed the hangers into the ground and hung a wind chime from each. Elinor watched him, blinking and twitching her tail, but he couldn't tell if she was judging him or approving of the addition.

"They'd probably be more impressive if there was any wind," he told the cat. "Or even a breeze. But they look cool, I guess."

Elinor didn't look impressed and, after watching the wind chimes do nothing for a long moment, he went into the house. The cat followed him and walked directly to her water dish. It was still full, but he'd gotten the message on day one that if she wanted fresh water, it was best to just refill the dish, even if he'd done it five minutes before she walked into the room.

He was nodding off in front of the television with Elinor curled up on the back of the couch and the top of his head when he realized the wind had picked up. "Hey, cat, let's go check out the wind chimes."

When she didn't move, he reached up and stroked her fur. She didn't like being petted while napping, so she'd move. He'd learned the hard way that if he just tried to get up, she'd feel like she was falling and scramble to save herself. With claws.

Once he was clear of her, he went toward the back of the house and he could hear the wind chimes before he pulled the slider open. They were louder and less melodious than they always sounded on TV and he wasn't surprised when Elinor sniffed and turned back for the couch.

Maybe they were better one at a time, and his mistake had been in putting all four out. He was halfway to the first one when he saw Meredith walking across her yard, and she didn't look happy.

She looked adorable, in pink sleep shorts with

a deeply V-necked tee and her hair gathered into a messy bun, but he got the impression she was trying to set him on fire with her eyeballs.

"Where did those come from?"

"What?"

"Those!" She pointed at the wind chimes barely on his side of the property line, each one swinging wildly on its decorative wrought-iron hook.

"I found them in the shed and decided to put them up. Aren't they soothing?"

"Soothing?" She laughed, but there was an edge to the sound, as if she was anxious about something bigger than some wind chimes. "No. No, they are not soothing."

"I'm pretty sure that's the reason they exist. To be soothing."

"What would be soothing is putting them back in the shed, where you found them."

She was cute when she was bossy, with her hands on her hips and her face all stern, but it wasn't going to work. "I like them where they are."

"So if I come out here and bang a metal spoon against a pan under your window at two o'clock in the morning, you're going to be okay with that?"

"No, that wouldn't be okay. Why would you do that to me?"

She looked as if she was trying not to laugh, even though she was clearly still annoyed with him. "To soothe you. Isn't that what you said metal banging against metal does?"

"There's a big difference between wind chimes and banging a metal pan."

"Not really. Metal clanging against metal. That's what they both are."

He narrowed his eyes. "How much did you have to drink when you were out with your friend?"

"I only had one drink and I made it last all through dinner. Trust me, not liking metal clanging in the wind outside my window has nothing to do with alcohol. And why, when we've been co-neighboring so well, did you decide to be annoying again *now*?"

He shrugged. "I found them tonight and needed some soothing, I guess."

"What upset you so much you had to go digging in the shed for decorative noise pollution?"

"I couldn't sleep." Cam wished he had the nerve to take out his phone and snap a photo of her right now, but he didn't think she'd appreciate it.

She threw her hands up in exasperation. "Maybe you can't sleep because you're still fully clothed and there's metal clanging in your yard."

That was a valid point, but she took a couple of steps forward and he got distracted by her legs again. She really did have great legs. But then he looked closer and saw a small trickle of what looked like blood on her shin.

"You have blood on your leg. Are you hurt?"

She looked down at her leg and then sighed. "It's nothing. I nicked myself shaving, and I thought it had stopped."

"Shaving your legs, huh? That's a fun thing to do when you have a sitter."

He watched her struggle not to laugh play out across her face, and eventually she lost. "Don't go getting any ideas over there."

"I've been having ideas since the day you moved in." It was a very blunt confession and he didn't, as a rule, like exposing his weak spots like that, but he was going to have to take the chance while he had it.

Whether it made things awkward between them or not, it was time to take his shot.

Chapter Thirteen

Meredith stood on her side of the yard, which was now separated from his by a line of clanking metal, with her hands on her hips and tried not to panic.

This was it. She had a sitter. She'd shaved her legs. And Cam was standing in front of her, dropping hints even she couldn't miss. If she was going to have sex with this sexy neighbor of hers, tonight was the night.

Stop thinking about it. Just do it.

As much as she appreciated Reyna's advice, she couldn't stop the thoughts racing around in her head. It was a big deal and once she got naked with this man, there was no going back.

And she couldn't handle having him in her bed. Maybe it didn't make sense, but she hadn't shared *her* bed with a man since her husband. And it was her home. Sophie's home. It felt like a much bigger deal to her.

But Cam had a bed. And he'd more or less just invited her into it. All she had to do was accept, but she was having a little trouble saying the words.

"You've been staring at me for a solid minute," Cam said, amusement obvious in his voice. "Let's rewind back to the blood on your leg. Carolina had a first-aid kit, so why don't you come in and let me clean it up for you."

It was a tiny nick, hardly worth the bother, but it got her inside the cottage, where it would be easier to fall into his bed. "That would be nice, thank you."

Before he went inside, he took the wind chimes off their hooks and laid them in the grass next to the hangers. "I'll put those away tomorrow."

"Maybe just one would be okay. But four on a windy night is a bit much, Cam."

He chuckled as they walked toward the cottage. "I had no idea they'd be that loud and it wasn't windy at all when I put them up. Believe it or not, I wasn't deliberately torturing you with my noise pollution."

Once they were inside, he told her to sit on the sofa and he went into the bathroom. Elinor leaped onto the cushion next to her and she stroked the cat's head, smiling when she kept headbutting Meredith's palm. She'd always thought cats were slightly strange, but she did like this one.

Except when she was tormenting Oscar. Cam and Elinor were a good match, she thought. Both could be really annoying neighbors at times, but also very sweet if they wanted to be.

Cam returned with a white plastic box bearing a first-aid label and pushed the coffee table away so he could kneel in front of her. It was nice to be fussed over once in a while, she mused as he ripped open the packaging on a cleaning wipe.

"Okay," he said with a frown, holding up the square inside. "I think this is supposed to be wet."

"They work better that way. Did you check the expiration date?"

"I didn't know they *had* expiration dates." He picked up the box and squinted at the label for a few seconds. "Oh, 1992. Thanks, Carolina."

She laughed at the expression on his face as he stared at the tiny bit of blood on her leg. The man was seriously vexed. "I promise it's not a big deal."

"Wait here."

He was gone only a minute, and then he returned with a paper towel he'd dampened the corner of. Kneeling in front of her, he dabbed carefully until the blood was gone.

With his other hand, he held the back of her calf,

and the feel of his hand on her body was enough to raise goose bumps on her skin. His grip was firm, but he was stroking her leg slightly with his thumb at the same time. She wasn't sure if it was meant to be comforting while he dealt with the almost non-existent cut, or if he was even aware he was doing it.

After he used the dry corner to make sure she wasn't still bleeding, he caressed the curve of her calf before letting her go. Then he tossed the paper towel into the first-aid kit and closed it with a snap.

"I'll be throwing that away," he said, his voice tight.

Stop thinking about it. Just do it.

Meredith leaned forward and ran her hand over his hair, her fingers threading through the thick strands. "Thank you for tending to my leg."

He froze for a second, then closed his eyes as she stroked the back of his head. "It was my pleasure."

There was probably a sexy quip to be made about *her* pleasure, but Meredith wasn't very good at sexy quips. Instead she curled her fingers in his hair and tugged slightly, so he got the hint.

As she leaned forward, he rose up on his knees and their mouths met halfway with a hunger that left no doubt she hadn't shaved her legs for nothing. His tongue danced over hers and she moaned against his mouth. His hands slid up her legs and cupped her hips for a moment before moving to her waist.

A harsh mewling sound from Elinor brought the kiss to an end. Meredith had forgotten she was there.

"Damn cat," Cam muttered. "I'd tell you to ignore her, but she doesn't like being ignored. She can be mean and has sharp claws, so if we make her mad, there might be more first aid in our future."

Before the part of her brain that liked to overthink things could catch up, Meredith went for it. "The bedroom has a door."

"You're sure?"

"I'm sure."

He stood and then took her hand to pull her up. Looking over her shoulder, he spoke to Elinor. "You stay right here or you and I are going to have a problem."

"You do remember that she's a cat, right?" she asked, chuckling as he pulled her toward the bedroom.

"Sometimes I wonder."

She watched him double-check that Elinor was still on the couch before closing the bedroom door. He had to push with his shoulder to make it click, and he even tugged on the doorknob to make sure the cat couldn't push it open.

Meredith looked at the clutter piled around the bedroom, including more pictures, paintings and embroideries on the wall than she could take in. Cam had carved out a small space for himself. The dresser top was clear of anything but his toiletries and a briefcase, and the bed had a plain gray comforter set on it that couldn't have belonged to Carolina.

"This is quite a room," she said as he pulled her into his arms.

"Close your eyes. Trust me, it helps."

She closed her eyes and was still chuckling when his mouth closed over hers. He kissed her slowly and thoroughly as his hands roamed over her back before coming to rest in her hair. Without breaking off the kiss, she reached up and pulled the scrunchie out of her hair so it tumbled down over his fingers.

Then she put a hand on his chest and broke off the kiss, opening her eyes. "This is probably a bad time to ask this, but do you have a condom?"

"I do. Several, in fact." He bent his head to nibble at her neck.

"You didn't find them in a drawer, did you?"

His laugh was like a puff of hot air across her skin. "No, they're mine. And I'm better than Carolina at tracking expiration dates."

"Oh, good. I didn't want to have to stop." She slid her hands under his shirt and reveled in the feel of his bare skin under her palms.

They explored each other's bodies as they kissed, slowly losing articles of clothing. Meredith felt a pang of self-consciousness when he tugged her panties down and she kicked them away, but it didn't last long as Cam stretched her out on the bed and kissed his way down her body.

It wasn't until he'd rolled on the condom and slowly entered her that she realized just how old the bed was. It squeaked as they moved, as if they were in a television sitcom, and when the headboard banged against the wall, she couldn't hold back the burst of laughter.

He dropped his head to her shoulder, his body shaking as he laughed with her. "I'd suggest we move to the couch, but Elinor's probably pissed we locked her out."

"No, it's fine. I just... I mean, *come on*. It's funny."

"At least I don't have any neighbors on that side. Nobody to call 9-1-1."

Trying to get her amusement under control, she cupped his face in her hands and pulled him in for a kiss. Then she captured his bottom lip between her teeth and he moaned.

She forgot all about the ancient bed when Cam moved his hips and the sensation she'd been craving since they met washed over her body. He kissed her as he moved, one of his thumbs brushing over her nipple, and her fingertips dug into the flexing muscles in his back.

When she cried out, arching under him, he buried his hand in her hair and murmured her name. And when he finally collapsed on top of her, he kissed her neck and her shoulder, his thumb caressing the side of her face.

"We didn't break the bed," he said once they were both breathing normally again.

"You sound surprised."

"I had my doubts, to be honest." He rolled off her, and sat on the edge of the bed. "I'll be right back."

The lights in the living room were still on, so when he opened the bedroom door, she saw that he'd pulled on boxer briefs. And that Elinor was sitting right outside the door, as if she'd been waiting for them.

"Excuse me, Your Highness," he said, stepping around her.

While he was gone, Meredith fished around on the floor and came up with Cam's T-shirt, which she slipped over her head. They passed in the doorway and she stood on her toes to give him a kiss. "Be right back."

"You're coming back to bed, right?" He reached down and stroked the outside of her thigh, making her shiver. "I'm not done with you."

"Assuming it doesn't collapse while I'm gone."

He chuckled. "Don't be too long, then."

After using the bathroom, Meredith turned out the lights and smiled at Elinor, who'd decided to curl up on the sofa for the night. She still closed the door, though, leaning into it to make sure it latched.

Then she crawled onto the bed and into Cam's arms. "How much do you think this bed can actually survive?"

He grinned and cupped her breast. "I don't know, but that sounds like a challenge to me."

Cam woke to something tickling his nose and for one horrifying second, he thought Elinor was flicking her tail in his face. Then he registered the warm weight curled against him and relaxed.

Meredith. She was in his bed and he didn't even care that her hair was tickling his face. He imagined some morning cuddle time, followed by drinking coffee on the back deck and watching the bay come to life. Breakfast, maybe. If he had any breakfast food in the house. As contentment flooded him, he kissed the top of her head.

And almost got a busted nose when she bolted upright. "What time is it?"

"Damn, Meredith. Do you wake up like this every morning?"

She clutched the sheet to her chest before turning her head to frown at him. "In your bed? No. Is there seriously no clock in here?"

"Seriously, there's no clock. I don't think Carolina worried much about the time, and I usually have my phone and watch on the nightstand next to the crochet doll hiding tissues under her dress and the blue glass jar of something I don't care to identify."

"It's probably vapor rub. You might not want to open that. And I *need* to know what time it is."

"I'm guessing about seven thirty."

She pulled the quilt up from the bottom of the bed and wrapped it around her before sliding out of bed, leaving him the sheet. "Did the wolves teach you to tell time like that when you were growing up out in the wilderness?"

"Wow, you are really sarcastic in the morning. I wouldn't have guessed that about you."

He sat up as she pulled open the door and almost tripped on the cat, who was sitting there again, looking as regal and demanding as usual. She went around Elinor, which dragged the quilt over the cat's fur and made her hiss, and Meredith didn't go far before she turned around and came back.

This time Elinor moved out of the way.

"What time is it?"

"Twenty after seven," she muttered.

"So I was right."

"It's *not* seven thirty."

He couldn't help it. He laughed at her, even though her annoyance with him was practically rolling off her like steam. She sighed and then started trying to pull on her clothes without dropping the quilt.

It was quite a show, and it did nothing to quell his amusement.

"I had you pegged as one of those chipper morning people," he said once he'd stopped laughing. "I guess not."

"I have to be home before Sophie. And you could help instead of laughing at me."

"You know what I think?" He threw back the sheet to get out of bed, not caring that he was naked. "I think you're trying to pick a fight with me so you have an excuse to storm out without doing the awkward morning-after dance."

She paused in the act of fastening her bra, which required her to drop the quilt entirely. "I'm not trying to pick a fight with you. And there's no awkward morning-after dance. Or no need for it to be awkward, I should say. We're both adults."

"Then stay and have coffee with me. We can drink it on the deck, and then I can watch you do your really short walk of shame."

Her face flushed pink for a few seconds, and then she finally laughed. It seemed to release some of the tension in her as she pulled her shirt on. "Sophie probably won't be home for hours. Coffee on the deck sounds nice, actually."

"We can have breakfast, too, if you like toast."

"I do like toast."

He grabbed her hand and pulled her close for a kiss. "I make really good toast."

"I can't wait."

Later, when they were sitting on his deck, drinking coffee and watching paddleboards out on the bay, Cam thought about it and couldn't remember when he'd ever had such a nice morning.

It was peaceful. Slow and lazy. And he was sharing it with Meredith.

"I don't want…" She started to say something, but stopped. It was a few seconds before she started again. "I don't want Sophie being confused by any of this. It was fun and maybe we'll do it again and maybe we won't, but it's best for us if nobody knows about it. Best for Sophie."

That certainly took some of the shine off his mood, but Cam nodded. "If you think it's best, then it's our secret."

"Thank you."

"But, Meredith?" He waited until she stopped staring at her coffee and looked at him. "I *am* going to want to do this again."

Her cheeks flushed. "Me, too."

Chapter Fourteen

One month later...

Meredith ducked just in time to avoid being clocked by a Wiffle Ball that went whizzing over her head.

"Sorry, Mommy!"

She laughed as her daughter ran by her to retrieve the wayward ball. "That was quite a hit. Now you just need to practice hitting it in the right direction."

"New rule," her dad called from across the yard. "If you hit Mom or Grandma, you're automatically out."

"It's almost time for cheese duty, anyway," Cam added. He was on grill duty since she still hadn't bought one and he'd been working on his barbecue skills. "Three more swings and then you've got to unwrap the slices for me, Sophie."

"What a beautiful day," her mom said. "Perfect for a backyard barbecue."

"Definitely." Especially when her contribution was sitting on her deck, doing nothing but dodging Wiffle Balls.

Meredith sipped her lemonade and watched Sophie hand the Wiffle Ball to her grandfather before standing on the piece of cardboard that was serving as home plate. They'd tried to explain to Sophie that she could put the ball on a stand to make it easier to hit, but she wanted none of that. She wanted the game she saw on television.

"Have I told you lately how happy I am you moved back?"

"I think it's been at least two days since the last time, Mom." She smiled. "But I'm happy, too. It was a big decision, but all I have to do is look at Sophie and I know it was the right one."

"And how lucky that Cam moved in just before you," Erin added.

Meredith stifled a groan. Here it came. "Technically he didn't move in. He's staying there temporarily."

"Summer's a long season. Things can change,"

her mom said, and she was smiling as she took a sip of her iced tea.

"Oops."

Meredith looked back to the Wiffle Ball game just in time to see the ball sail out over the dock and land in the water.

"Well, that's a foul ball," her father reported drily.

"It floats," Sophie said. "Can we get it, Grandpa?"

"I have a fishing pole in my truck," he said. "I guess it's time to teach you how to fish."

"Mommy, can you do the cheese? Me and Grandpa have to learn fishing for my Wiffle Ball."

Meredith pushed herself to her feet. "What do you think the chances are Sophie's going to fall in and Dad's going to have to jump in after her?"

Erin laughed. "I'm betting on your father *thinking* Sophie's about to fall in and making a grab for her, then she doesn't fall in but he does."

Meredith was still laughing when she reached Cam's side, and she pulled a slice of cheese out of the package on the grill shelf.

"Will you still be laughing when you have to haul her out of the lake?"

"Absolutely. She can swim and my dad's the one who's going to have to haul her out." She peeled the wrapper off the cheese and leaned past him to place it on a burger.

"She loves spending time with them."

"That she does. They talked a lot on the phone and did video chats, but it's not the same. Being able to spend so much time together this summer has brought them even closer, and it's been so good for Sophie."

"Any chance she's going to go home with them?"

She laughed and placed another slice of cheese. "No, they're not taking her home with them."

"Maybe they'll be so tired after a long day of Wiffle Ball and accidental swimming that they'll just crash at your place?"

"Doubtful. But never give up hope," she teased.

Finding alone time with a six-year-old underfoot during summer vacation wasn't easy, and they'd managed it only a few times over the last month. A sleepover with her grandparents. One sleepover at Kiki's house. And two afternoon quickies while Sophie was with Kiki's mom at summer program events.

Cam was good about it, though. He understood that she was very sensitive about Sophie's attachment to him, and he hadn't yet visited Meredith's bed. Sophie still remembered climbing into Meredith and Devin's bed early in the mornings, and she was afraid finding Cam in that position would lead to a whole lot of questions there were no answers or easy explanations for.

Another reason, which she hadn't shared with

Cam, that the current arrangement worked was that it was something of a built-in braking system for their relationship. Stolen interludes at his place helped her remember that she and Cam were just enjoying each other's company. It wouldn't end anywhere but with him back in the city.

The summer was almost over. Labor Day was coming in two and a half weeks, and Sophie started school the following Tuesday. The long holiday weekend was the unofficial end of summer and, while there was still a lot of work to be done with the cottage, it had become the date the countdown clock in her subconscious was ticking down toward.

Maybe he'll change his mind.

It was a thought that kept popping up more and more often, but she did her best to squash it each time. He wasn't going to change his mind about having an amazing life in the city to move to Blackberry Bay and…do what? Besides Meredith and Sophie, he had nothing here. And there were no promises between them. Just some fun.

"You look very serious all of a sudden."

Cam's voice jerked her out of her thoughts and she laughed off his concern. "No, just lost in thought for a minute."

"You also stopped putting cheese on the burgers, so they're not all going to melt the same way."

"They'll be fine," she said, loving how the grill brought out a need to succeed in him.

They managed to get lunch served with acceptable cheeseburgers, and Sophie and her grandfather were both still dry after retrieving the Wiffle Ball, so Meredith counted that as a win.

Under the table, Cam's leg pressed against hers, and she savored the warm contact of his body. It was the only touching they'd do with her parents and Sophie present, which was frustrating even though it was at her request. She wasn't ready to make things more confusing for Sophie.

"Cam, how are things going with the cottage?" Erin asked when they'd pushed away empty plates and leaned back in their chairs.

"Slow," he admitted. "I should probably spend more time in the cottage and less time in my hammock. Tomorrow I'm going to dig into the last box of journals, though. I'm getting there. I guess if I was smart I would read the journals while *in* the hammock."

They all laughed, but Meredith suspected the truth behind the joke. He was dragging his feet on the process, and while he talked about how overwhelming it was, she knew that wasn't all there was to it. For one thing, he could afford to have all the help he wanted. And he could box up the journals and take them with him to read later. That wasn't the task he should be doing if he was trying to finish up the estate work.

He was getting attached to Carolina's belongings. She could see it in the way he'd pick something up and hold it, his gaze shifting to the pictures that were still hanging on the walls. The journal entries. The ridiculous Chihuahua tablecloth that was still on the table. They were all pieces of the puzzle that was his grandmother and, even though there would probably always be missing pieces, he wasn't ready to sweep them all into boxes and put that puzzle on the shelf.

It seemed to her as though he wasn't ready to go back to New York. Maybe he didn't want to go back to what sounded to her like a cold and sometimes awful relationship with his parents. Or Carolina and Michael could be holding him in Blackberry Bay. Leaving would be like putting them in his rearview mirror and he might not be ready to let them go yet.

There was also the possibility he was reluctant to leave her. Maybe he was having as hard a time imagining his life without her and Sophie in it as she was picturing her life without him.

She'd gotten used to having him around. Sure, it was weird having a secret relationship with her neighbor, but they still spent a good part of their days together. There was a lot of playing with Sophie in the backyard. They'd spend time helping him in the cottage. They were all working on taming Carolina's garden patches together. They'd eat on one of the decks together at least three nights of the week.

It was times like this that made it hard. They were beginning to feel like a family to her, and it was only when she snuck him a kiss good-night and sent him home alone before putting Sophie to bed that shattered the illusion.

And if they felt like a family to her, they probably felt like a family to Sophie, and with each passing week, her concern grew. It was impossible to keep them apart, though. All Sophie had to do was see Cam and she was across the yard like a shot.

The only boundary she could maintain was not having Cam fill the role of the man of *her* house. They ate on the deck. He never slept in her bed. It wasn't much, but hopefully it would help when the inevitable separation came.

His knee bumped hers and she looked at him. His brow was furrowed and he tilted his head in a questioning way. *What's wrong?*

She should have sat on the other side of the table from him. Smiling, she shook her head and tried to focus on the conversation going on around her, which seemed to center around Sophie's friendship with Kiki. They'd found out they'd be in the same class and, judging by her daughter's enthusiasm for the subject, it was the best thing that had ever happened to her.

It was her mother's smile that really caught her attention. She wasn't beaming at her granddaughter. Her gaze was bouncing between Cam and Meredith, and there was no mistaking the look in her eyes.

Great, Meredith thought. They didn't just feel like a family. They looked like one, too.

Today at the library, I learned how to search in the Google and I searched for my grandson. There are some pictures of him on the internet and it both hurts my heart and makes me happy at the same time that he looks so much like my Michael. Some of the pictures have his parents in them and, in those, none of them ever look happy. They smile, but they don't look like real smiles. And I know my grandson's aren't. He has Michael's eyes and I could always tell by his eyes when he smiled if it was real or not. My grandson looks like he's playing a part in a movie he didn't ask to be cast in and maybe he just needs to know he can quit if he wants to. He can find another role to play that suits him better.

I swore to Michael I would never interfere. I promised him I would go to my grave without ever revealing the truth and I'll honor that promise. Technically. I'll be buried before my grandson gets the letter.

Cam closed the journal and then shut his eyes against the wave of emotions. First, the familiar anger at his mother. The sense of regret and loss. But then he laughed, startling Elinor, who'd curled up at his side. She gave him an affronted look and then went back to sleep.

Carolina really was something else.

Now he had the answer to one of the questions that had simmered in the back of his mind all through this adventure—why, if she was going to blow up his life, didn't she do it while she was still alive so he could at least get to know her?

Because she'd made a promise to her son and that letter from her lawyer was the only way she could see around it.

Before he could talk himself out of it, he pulled up the information the lawyer had given him and punched the number for Tess Weaver into his phone. He was finally ready to talk to somebody who'd really known her well, and from what he understood, nobody had known her better than Tess.

An hour later, Cam sat at the most private table he could find in the café, fighting the urge to rub his palms on his thighs. When he'd called her, he hadn't expected things to move quite so fast, but Tess seemed to prefer not letting grass grow under her feet.

He'd met some of the most powerful people in the

country. He dined regularly with senators and he'd gone to school with people who now kept the private jet industry in business. And he'd never once felt out of his depth.

But as an older woman with long gray hair hanging in a braid over her shoulder, wearing jeans with a sparkly pink T-shirt and matching sneakers, walked in, he felt as anxious as he'd ever felt going into a meeting.

Sophie would love her outfit, he thought, but then the woman spotted him and froze. For a few seconds, she simply stared, and then she seemed to gather herself and moved toward him. He stood to greet her.

"I wasn't prepared for how much you look like Michael," she said, holding out her hand for him to shake. "I'm Tess Weaver."

"Cam." He gestured to the chair across the table from his. "Please, sit down. And thank you for agreeing to see me."

"I've been waiting. To be honest, I'd about given up hope you were going to reach out, so I'm glad you did."

"It's been a lot to deal with," he admitted. "I didn't know anything about her or Michael until I got the letter, so I've been trying to come to grips with it all. And I'm not one who likes to talk things out. But I guess there are some things you can never totally wrap your head around."

"I promised Carolina I wouldn't interfere at all. If you'd chosen to send somebody to throw everything away and sell off the cottage, then that's all that was going to happen. And if, by chance, you did come yourself, she asked me to let you be unless and until you wanted to know more and started asking questions."

"I have her journals," he said. "I wouldn't say I've found specific answers to questions, but I've gotten to know a lot about her and quite a bit about her son from reading them. I'm sorry I never got to meet her."

Tess's smile was sad, but her eyes warmed. "I'm sorry, too. She loved being a grandmother, which sounds ridiculous since she never got to see you, but she liked knowing you were out there."

Emotion clogged Cam's throat, so all he could do was nod. The server showing up to take their orders gave him a couple of minutes to compose himself, so by the time they'd each ordered the pasta salad special and drinks, he was ready to talk again.

But he didn't have to worry about talking because Tess liked to talk and she talked fast, even for a New Englander. She told so many stories about her adventures with Carolina—only some of which he knew from her journals—that he knew he'd never keep them straight in his head.

"When my mom left," he said when she finally took a breath, "how did that play out?"

"She just left." Tess shrugged. "Michael told Carolina she was keeping the baby but she was going back to her husband and the baby would have a good life. Michael signed off on it and swore Carolina to secrecy. She didn't like it, but Michael was sure in his heart it was best for you."

"So he just let her go? Just let *me* go? Just like that."

"He knew who Melissa's husband was and he wasn't going to win. He couldn't afford a lawyer, never mind a lawyer who could fight the Maguire family, so all it was going to do was bring you into a world of conflict and anger."

What about the money? The question burned in his mind, but he couldn't bring himself to ask it. Tess not mentioning the check made him wonder if Carolina had even known about it. What if Michael had accepted the money and never told anybody about it?

Maybe his biological father *hadn't* been a good guy. That was the problem with Carolina's journals. Everything he knew about Michael Archambault was filtered through the eyes of a loving mother.

"So I hear you're running around with Erin Lane's girl. So sad about her husband, but it's good she's moved home again so she can be near her mom." Tess paused. Frowned. "I probably shouldn't have asked about you dating her and talked about her husband in the same breath."

He tried to catch up with her conversational curve-ball. "We're not dating. And Meredith is comfort-able talking about her husband. It sounds like he was a great guy and it is sad, for both her and Sophie."

"You're not dating?" Her skepticism couldn't have been more obvious, but he was determined to hold the line. Meredith wanted their business kept very private and he wasn't going to blow it. "Rumor has it you kissed her right in the middle of the sidewalk after the fireworks so people trying to get back to their cars had to walk out around you."

Cam couldn't help laughing at her description. "That's a little dramatic. I did kiss her, yes. There's not much sense in denying it, since everybody in this town seems to know about it. But that doesn't mean we're dating."

"Guess you're not much of a kisser, then, huh?"

"I…" Nonplussed, he shut his mouth and just blinked at her until she laughed.

He had no intention of telling this woman he and Meredith had progressed to a lot more than kissing when opportunity knocked, which wasn't often. But he was okay with that because it made their time alone together all the sweeter.

"Just kidding with you. And it's none of my busi-ness, anyway." She shrugged and stabbed her fork into a cherry tomato. "It's probably for the best you're not dating because, last I heard, you haven't made Carolina's cottage your permanent address."

He was tempted to ask how she would know anything about that. But he didn't bother. Blackberry Bay seemed to be the kind of town where everybody seemed to know things—or thought they did, at least—and they weren't shy about sharing the info with each other.

"Do you know anybody who might be interested in some of Carolina's things?" he asked, determined to get the conversation back on track. "She liked crafts. And…well, she liked a *lot* of things."

Tess laughed. "That she did. Boy, you need to have yourself a yard sale. The long Labor Day weekend would be perfect. And don't you worry. I'll help."

Cam stifled the groan that seemed to rise up in him from the very depths of his soul. A yard sale.

Great.

Chapter Fifteen

"How many books did you get, Cam?"

They were sitting on the grass in the park, eating ice cream after a trip to the library, as they did once a week. Meredith and Sophie were there several times each week, thanks to the summer reading program, but Cam only accompanied them once because there was only one ice cream per week.

"I only got one," he said, showing Sophie the hardcover thriller he had stashed in his tote.

"Just one? What are you going to do when you finish it?"

"I'm pretty busy, so I don't have a lot of reading time right now."

And he'd be leaving soon, and he couldn't take Spurr Memorial Library's books with him. The thought blindsided Meredith and she sucked in a breath. They both looked at her, but she forced a smile.

"Brain freeze," she lied, holding up the ice-cream cone to back her claim.

"Can we go down on the dock?" Sophie asked. "I'm all done with mine."

"I am, too." He nodded his head toward Meredith. "Your mom's slow."

"She says she likes to *savor* it." Her impression of her mother was very dramatic and they all laughed.

"You guys go. I'm going to stay here and savor my ice cream since, unlike you two, I still have some."

Cam held up his hand and Sophie pulled on it, laughing when he made a big show out of struggling to stand up. She was chattering like usual as they walked away, with Sophie skipping a couple of steps ahead, and Meredith watched them go with a full heart.

She'd just popped the last bite of cone into her mouth when her cell phone chimed. She dug it out of the tote and found a text message from Reyna.

Caramel apple guy wants me to meet his sister. Help.

Meredith chuckled as she typed in a response. Poor Lucas. It didn't matter how long he dated

Reyna. They were always going to call him the caramel apple man.

That sounds less serious than meeting his parents, and you've been dating long enough for a sibling.

His parents live in the Midwest, so I can't meet them without staying with them. That's a long way off. But I don't know if I want to meet his sister. That's a big commitment.

Isn't commitment what you're hoping for?

It took Reyna longer to respond this time, so she'd either been interrupted or she was giving serious thought to the question. Knowing her friend, probably the former.

Fine. I'll meet his sister. I'll tell you when so we can have lunch after. Or drinks. Probably drinks.

Keep me posted.

After dropping the phone back in her tote, she looked across the park for Cam and Sophie, hoping he wasn't sending some kind of signal to her, begging to be rescued from her energetic chatterbox of a daughter. But he wasn't.

She wasn't sure her heart could take the sight of

Cam and Sophie sitting side by side on the dock, their legs dangling over the water, while she pointed at something in the distance.

Over the last few weeks, it felt as if the countdown clock to Cam leaving had been ticking faster and faster in her head. She'd failed at not falling for him. She'd failed at keeping some distance between him and Sophie. And that was on her. She'd gotten herself and her daughter through a devastating loss before. She could do it again.

When several kids on bikes wheeled into the park, Sophie got up and ran toward them. Meredith could tell by the way they greeted her they knew her, and she thought she recognized two of them from summer reading program events.

Cam made his way back to Meredith and sat on the grass beside her. "I've been traded in for the younger crowd."

"She'll know quite a few of the kids before school starts, so that's a good thing." She sighed. "And it's right around the corner. My baby's going to be in first grade."

"That sounds like a good reason for cupcakes."

She wondered if he'd be around to eat them. "Speaking of school starting, which means Labor Day, have you given any more thought to the yard sale idea?"

He groaned. "I know I have to, but I really don't want to."

"We'll help you. And you said Tess Weaver told you she and some of Carolina's other friends will help, too. You really need to get it done and behind you."

"Do you know how long it will take to put price stickers and tags on everything in that house?" he asked. "I think we would have had to start in 2006 to be done by Labor Day."

"So only price the larger items and things with an obvious value. Let people make an offer on all the other stuff, and you can group similar things in a bundle. Like, fill a bag with yarn instead of selling individual skeins."

"You sound like a woman with exemplary yard sale management skills."

She laughed and swatted at his shoulder. "Nope. This is your show, Cam. I'll help behind the scenes, but I'm not running your yard sale."

"I'll call Tess and ask her to help. I have a feeling once I call her, this yard sale's going to be a runaway train and I wouldn't be able to back out if I wanted to."

"I think you're right about that. I've seen this kind of thing in Blackberry Bay before, and it's no joke. We might have to hire a traffic cop."

He looked at her, eyes wide. "Seriously?"

"No. *That* part was a joke. But I think you'll be pleased with the results."

"It would be good to have that part done," he said, and then he seemed content to watch Sophie playing with the kids.

"I can't believe it's almost Labor Day, though," she said quietly, because she couldn't stop herself.

"I know. Summer's almost over."

The way he said it and the long silence that drew out between them told Meredith the impending holiday weekend was weighing heavily on his mind, as well. At some point they were going to have to talk about what was happening between them. The wondering and hoping and trying *not* to hope was taking a toll on her.

"I guess you'll be leaving soon," she finally forced out.

He inhaled slowly before blowing out the breath. "I don't know what's happening. I mean, the cottage isn't anywhere near ready to sell and… I guess things are still up in the air."

It was enough for now. He was wavering and she didn't want to push too hard and force him into a corner. If he decided he was going to stay in Blackberry Bay, she wanted it to be a decision he'd come to on his own. She wanted him to *want* to stay.

"We have to get going, honey," she called to Sophie, signaling an end to that conversation before she got to her feet. "I'm trying to get better about dinner and bedtimes now that school is looming on the horizon. It's hard when it's not dark yet."

He stood up and brushed the grass off his shorts. "Some room-darkening shades might help. I have those in my apartment."

It was tempting to ask him what his apartment looked like. Maybe being able to visualize what his life looked like in the city would help when it came to keeping her hopefulness in check. But Sophie was already back with them, picking up her tote bag of books.

"I might order a set," was all she said, and then they started walking toward where she'd parked.

I guess you'll be leaving soon.

For the last week, all he'd been able to think about when he was alone were Meredith's words at the park.

He *should* be leaving soon. If he wanted to be real with himself, he should have been gone a long time ago. He could have stripped the cottage of personal items and the journals and let somebody else deal with the rest.

And if he wanted to be *really* real with himself, he'd admit it wasn't his family or Carolina keeping him here. Yes, he'd enjoyed learning about his grandmother, and he hoped to embrace her philosophies of joy and love as he went through the rest of his life.

But he wasn't in a hurry to leave because he was struggling to imagine having joy and love for the rest of his life without Meredith in it. Without Sophie.

He hadn't been in a hurry to find a woman to settle down and start a family with. He wasn't *opposed* to marriage, but he'd always had a hard time imagining himself as a husband and father. Maybe it was growing up with parents who hid a lot of unhappiness behind polite smiles, but the urge for his own family hadn't exactly been at the forefront of his mind.

The idea of being a stepfather was…simply terrifying. Not only would he have to learn to love a child with a lot more heart than his father had loved him, but Sophie wasn't his. And she'd known and would forever miss the love of a man who sounded like a really great dad.

It was a lot of pressure.

He was a man who usually worked best under pressure, thanks to his father. But if he was wrong— if he and Meredith *weren't* the real thing—he could do a lot of emotional damage to a little girl who'd already been through a lot.

And to himself. If he took the leap and was wrong, he wasn't sure he could recover. Meredith hadn't invited him into their lives fully. She hadn't invited him into *her* bed. And she hadn't asked him to stay in Blackberry Bay.

His gut told him it was wrong, but the possibility existed she was just enjoying his company because she'd been alone a long time and he'd be leaving at the end of the summer. He was safe. But he didn't think so.

"You're going to be having this yard sale in the house at the rate you're going," Meredith said, walking by him with an armload of folded fabric.

He shook away the what-if thoughts and pointed at her load. "What is all that for?"

"Based on some of the stuff I found with this, I think Carolina went through a very brief but well-stocked quilting phase." She paused, looking at him thoughtfully. "I just realized when my husband died, I was only three years younger than Carolina was when she lost her husband."

"Do you want all the quilting stuff?"

She laughed, rolling her eyes. "No, I do not want to take up quilting. Or knitting or counted cross-stitch or… Actually, I've always wanted to learn to knit. But I'm not taking all this. I'll start small. But she must have been lonely. That's a long time to be alone."

"I guess she never found anybody else she loved as much as her husband. My grandfather. And she had Elinor."

"I don't think Elinor's that old." She frowned. "Do we know how old Elinor is?"

"Believe it or not, she's only six. I'd call her a rescue, but according to the journal entry, she just showed up and moved in. I'm not sure Carolina had a lot of say in the matter. So the age is approximate, I guess, but that's what the vet records say."

"I hope she had other pets before Elinor, to keep her company." She dropped the fabric on top of an existing pile. "And maybe she chose not to get married again. Though I don't know that you'd love again in the same way. You'd love differently, because it would be a different man. A different relationship."

She was looking out the window as she spoke, and he wasn't sure if she was talking in vague terms about Carolina, or if she was talking about herself. About how she would love a man differently from the way she loved her husband.

Maybe she loved *him*.

His pulse quickened as hope surged through him. Maybe they'd finally talk about what was going on between them. He couldn't make a decision like this without all the facts, and whether or not she even wanted a future with him was a pretty important piece of information not on the table.

Then she looked at him and took a slow breath. He held his, waiting for her to speak, but he saw the moment pass in her eyes and she shrugged. "You didn't leave Elinor's vet records buried in a box, did you?"

"No, they're in an envelope with her name on it on the counter, so they don't get mixed up with everything else." Apparently they were just going to keep on going as they had been.

For now.

A burst of laughter from outside caught their attention and he moved closer to her so he could see out the window.

Tess and some of her friends, along with Meredith's friend Reyna and her mother, were setting up a boatload of folding tables they'd borrowed from the church. Usually they held all the slow cookers a Blackberry Bay potluck dinner required, but Tess had decided they'd be perfect for a yard sale of this magnitude.

The reason for the laughter seemed to be Sophie, who had one hand on her hip—looking very much like her mother—and was directing the women with her free hand.

"I should go rescue them," Meredith said, scooping up the towering pile of fabric.

"I hope all this work is worth it," he said, stepping forward to take the heavy stack from her. "I don't know what I'd do without all this help."

"That's the nice thing about a town like Black-

berry Bay. There's always somebody willing to help."
She chuckled. "Whether you want it or not."

She held the door for him, since his arms were full
of fabric, and he managed to get out the door without
tripping over Oscar or Elinor. It was a very warm
day, but that didn't seem to be slowing down the
women who'd begun arranging things on the tables.

"What are we going to do if it rains?" he asked,
setting the fabric down on one of the tables.

"That's why we have tarps," Tess said, putting
her hands on her hips as she surveyed the tables.
"Haven't you ever done a yard sale before?"

"No, I can't say that I have."

"He'd never had a library card before, either," Sophie volunteered. "Mommy had to help him get one."

"At least he's got one now," Tess said over the
laughter around them.

Setting up a yard sale was a lot of work, with
women going in and out of the cottage all day. He
and Meredith had moved his few belongings into the
bedroom along with the boxes of journals and a few
other things he wasn't sure about yet.

The rest of it was brought outside for display or, in
some cases, put in a pile to go to the dump. He'd also
told everybody helping they were welcome to keep
anything they wanted to, so more than a few trips
were made to the cars parked along the road, too.

The cottage was emptying out fast, and when he

went inside to get the burgers and dogs for the grill—the least he could do was feed his volunteers—he was struck by the fact it wouldn't be long before it was *actually* empty.

He looked at the photo of his biological father hanging on the wall. The one that was almost, though not quite, like looking in a mirror. Every night he read more of Carolina's journals, and every night he got more answers to his questions. One thing had become very clear to him over the last couple of nights, and that was that Michael Archambault *was* a good man. A very good man, and Cam was always going to regret not having met him.

He'd needed the money. Or rather, Carolina had needed it because she got sick, and Michael had two battles on his hands. Tess was right about the fact he wouldn't have won against the Maguires. But he could save his mother.

"Are you okay?" Meredith's arms slid around his waist, and she pressed her cheek to his back.

"I am now," he said, covering her interlocked hands with his and pushing thoughts of Michael to the back of his mind. "Just taking in the echo, I guess. I didn't think we'd ever get through it all. Hopefully everything sells because I don't want to have to bring it all back in."

"It'll sell. And Tess said if there was stuff left over at the end of Sunday, she'd spread the word it's free for the taking the next morning and, trust me, people will be like locusts. You'll be lucky if your car's still here by noon Monday."

"I hope you're right. Except, you know, the part about my car. I need that."

After a quick squeeze, her arms fell away and she wasn't smiling when she stepped past him. "I promise, a ton of people are going to show up tomorrow and Sunday."

It took him a few seconds to realize that it was his comment about needing his car that had changed the mood so suddenly. The fact he was supposed to be leaving soon wasn't a black cloud looming off in the distance anymore. It was over them now, casting shade over their days.

They were going to talk about it soon, he promised himself. Because if nothing else, he knew two things.

Things couldn't continue as they were. He needed to close out Carolina's estate and close that chapter. And he had angry parents waiting for him in New York City with growing impatience. There were loose ends that had to be tied up.

And he was 100 percent in love with Meredith Price.

Chapter Sixteen

"I think that's the last of it."

Cam looked around the yard and back at Meredith, finding it hard to believe. "We did it?"

"There are still a lot of personal belongings in the house. The stuff that Tess said she and her friends would go through and give away to people they knew would want it. And the important documents and all that. But the extra stuff is all gone, so the yard sale was definitely a success."

"And as soon as these ladies are done, it'll be officially over." Cam looked at the two women who'd piled their purchases around a very small car and had spent the last five minutes trying to fit it all in like puzzle pieces. He'd offered to help, but they assured him they did this all the time.

"Just in time, too," Meredith said. "My parents will be dropping Sophie off any minute, so I'm going to take the money box inside and sort it while I wait. You can break down the folding tables."

"Yes, ma'am." He wanted to kiss her, but they still had an audience, so he held himself to appreciating the view as she walked inside.

He was folding the last of the tables when a black Cadillac SUV pulled up in front of the house, parking on the side of the road. Not paying much attention to it—they'd be able to see the yard sale was over—he leaned the table against the others.

"Good lord," a woman snapped from behind him and the voice turned his insides to ice.

"Mom?"

"Hello, Calvin," she said, and his back stiffened. She'd deliberately set the tone by opening with the name she knew he loathed.

She was wearing a black pantsuit with her typical high-heeled shoes, with her dark hair pulled into a sleek ponytail, showing off the ridiculously large diamonds in her ears. Obviously she didn't care how much she stood out in a small town on a warm holiday weekend. Or maybe that was why she did it. Even her clothing choices were power moves.

Not wanting to give the two ladies putting the

last of the bags into their car anything to talk about over lunch, he gestured for her to follow and went into the house. He could see Meredith standing at the counter, banding together bundles of dollar bills, but he couldn't focus on her right now.

"How did you find me?" he demanded from his mother. Her expression told him that question was utterly ridiculous, and anger churned in his gut. "How long have you known I was in Blackberry Bay?"

"You're my son. I know that if you're determined to do something—no matter how foolish—you're going to do it and trying to stop you will only push you harder. You were behaving very unlike yourself and it didn't take me long to figure it out, so I've known for most of the summer where you were and why. What I don't know is what exactly you're doing with this situation."

He looked around, thinking it was fairly obvious. "I had a yard sale."

"A yard sale." She put a finger to her temple and rubbed for a moment, as if the concept of her child having a yard sale was something she couldn't process.

"What are you doing here?"

"Your father's patience with your absence has come to an end." Maybe it was just his imagination, but it sounded as if she stressed the word *fa-*

ther. "Naturally, he's blaming me for this situation, so I've come to bring you home where you belong."

As she said the last words—*where you belong*—she turned her head to look at Meredith, who was watching them with concern and confusion clouding her expression. "And is this my future daughter-in-law?"

Cam's brain froze for a few seconds as he panicked, not sure how his mother could have known about his feelings for Meredith and that he'd been spending more and more time thinking about how they could have a future together.

And then he remembered the lie he'd told his parents when he got the letter from Carolina's lawyer—that he was going to spend the summer with a prospective wife's family. She'd known practically the entire time that it was a lie, so the question was a deliberate move to remove a potential obstacle to getting what she wanted—Cam back in New York City so they could pretend this summer never happened.

She was looking at Meredith when she asked the question, but there was no warmth or welcome in her tone or expression. Just a cold, judgmental assessment that had Meredith's wide eyes locking with his.

"No, and you know it," he said to his mother, and Meredith's gaze narrowed. She was probably in the process of jumping to the conclusion he had a fiancée he hadn't told her about. And there wasn't a thing he could do to assure her that wasn't the case while his mother was in the room. "This is my neighbor, Meredith Price. Meredith, my mother, Melissa Maguire."

"Your neighbor." She nodded sharply, then turned away from Meredith, dismissing her. "The yard sale had me wondering if you'd lost all sense and were actually considering staying here."

"Of course not," he snapped, lashing out against the accusation he'd lost all sense.

But he saw Meredith's face when he said the words—the color draining away as her lips parted slightly from the shock. His mind, shaken by his mother's arrival, scrambled to come up with words that could explain what he'd meant.

She didn't wait for an explanation. "Obviously you two have a lot to talk about. What a *pleasure* to meet you, Mrs. Maguire. Goodbye, Cam."

She turned and walked out the door, her spine stiff and her chin high, and Cam itched to run after her. But there was no use in that as long as his mother was still in this house. Once he got rid of her, he could make things right with Meredith.

Goodbye.

It was the first time she'd ever used that word, he realized. *Good night. See you later. See you in the morning.* Never *goodbye.*

One problem at a time.

"You did that deliberately," he said, the accusation leaving his lips in a tone that could have cut through granite.

"Did what deliberately?"

"You knew I was here, and you know *why*. So you threw my lie about being involved with a woman at me and baited me just to get rid of Meredith."

"I don't want anything—or anybody—holding you here. This is done and now it's time to take your rightful place at your father's side." She held up her hand as he opened his mouth to speak. "The father who raised you and has given you everything in life."

"Everything?" He chuckled, but it was a sound totally without mirth. After spending the summer in Blackberry Bay, he knew exactly what Calvin III *hadn't* given him. "Everything money could buy, you mean."

"He accepted you as his own, and he didn't have to."

Cam looked at his mother for a long moment, wondering if she actually believed that or if keeping up the pretense was something she was compelled to do. "The worst thing is not knowing if he can't show me love because he's incapable of it or because I'm not really his son."

"You *are* his son, in all ways that matter," she snapped. "And he deserves better than this, so go pack your personal belongings. We have people who can handle the disposition of everything else."

He recognized the dismissal in the way she lifted her chin and turned to walk away, but then her gaze snagged on the framed photo of Michael Archambault hanging over the armchair and she nearly stumbled. Cam reached out a hand with the intent of catching her, but she steadied herself.

She didn't look away, though. He felt the seconds ticking by as she stared at the face of the man she'd known so long ago. And for the first time, she looked vulnerable to her son. He saw the cracks in her hard veneer and the surprising sheen of tears in her eyes. A slight tremor of her hair gave away the fact she was trembling slightly, and he almost stepped forward to put his arms around her.

But then she sniffed once as her spine straightened and, just like that, his mother was back to her typical self.

"It's time to come home, Calvin," she said, and the use of his given name again told him she meant business. And her tone was more brittle than usual, even for her. "This business is finished and it's time to put it behind you. The car service will drop me at that shabby, overpriced inn next to the public docks and then be dismissed, so when you're ready you may pick me up there. Please don't keep me waiting long."

He stood in the same spot for at least two minutes after she'd gone, trying to process the swirl of emotions running through him. Shock that this day had played out this way. Fear for the hurt they'd caused Meredith. Anger that his mother was moving him around like a pawn on a chessboard.

Going back to New York was a given at this moment. As tempting as it was to let his mother sit at the inn until it became her permanent address, this wouldn't stop until he stopped it. He had to deal with his family and their expectations. And he had to figure out how he could make the life waiting for him and the life Meredith wanted blend into one.

He'd talk to her before he left. He'd do his best to make her understand his anger at his mother had twisted his words into something he hadn't meant. But right now, with his emotions running high and anger still leading the way, probably wasn't the time.

Packing first, he thought. A mindless activity that would allow him time to cool off so he could have a clear head when he tried to convince Meredith he was going to come back. That he wasn't walking out on her.

"You came back."

"One of the more inconvenient things about being a parent is that it's almost impossible to have a private conversation in your own house." She stepped inside just far enough to close the slider behind her. "She's talking to my mom on video chat right now, even though they got home from dropping her off not too long ago, just so I could get a few minutes."

"I can explain."

"That's why I'm here." It was probably her imagination, but it seemed as if she could still feel the chill in the air his mother had left in her wake.

"I told them I was spending the summer at a lake house with a prospective wife so I could get to know her family."

"Prospective wife? Are you kidding me?" She couldn't believe somebody in this century would actually use that phrase. "And they believed you? Had you been dating somebody that seriously? Do you have a girlfriend waiting for you back in the city right now?"

"No." He stepped toward her, but she crossed her arms and shook her head to keep him at bay. She couldn't deal with him touching her right now. "I was single when I got here, and had been for a while. I lied to them, but not to you. I've never really shared details of my personal life with my parents and, at that point, I think all my dad cared about was that the fake woman I was dating came from a family who maintained an out-of-state summer home."

"I'm sorry you and your family aren't close. I really am. But you *did* lie to me, Cam."

"I've never told you anything that isn't true." He sighed. "And when I said 'of course not,' I was referring to losing my sense, not what my mother said. I didn't mean that how it sounded."

"It's not what you've said. It's what you *haven't* said." Unable to bear looking at him, she looked away, and that was when she spotted the luggage and boxes stacked in front of the stove. "You're leaving. You're actually going."

"I have to. I've pushed my parents as far as I can, and it's time."

"Were you going to tell us?"

"Of course I was." He pushed his hand through his hair, blowing out a breath. "You knew I was here for the summer."

There it was. The blunt reminder that she'd gotten her own self into this mess. She *had* known all along he was only here for the summer, and the fact she'd begun hoping his plans were changing—that he might decide to stay—wasn't his fault.

He hadn't lied to her. She'd lied to herself.

"I did know that," she said quietly.

"Maybe I can come back. I need to get things straightened out but I can come back and—"

"And what? Your life is in New York City. You're always going to have to be there, and Sophie and I are very happy here. It was a fun summer. Drive safe and have a good life."

"Meredith, don't. Please."

"I'm going back to my daughter and you're going

back to New York. It's over." She grabbed an envelope off the counter and then pulled open the slider before turning back to face him with the last reserve of strength she could muster. "And we're keeping the cat."

There was no way to slam a sliding glass door, so she didn't get to punctuate her exit as strongly as she wanted to, but she could still feel the finality as it slid home in her hand.

She scooped Elinor off the deck rail as she left, and she was surprised she managed to make it down the deck's steps and across the lawn without tripping. Tears were burning her eyes, and she had to stop and wipe them away before she went inside.

"Mommy's back," she heard Sophie tell her grandmother. "Mommy, do you want to talk to Grandma?"

"Not right now." She was amazed her voice sounded so steady. "Tell her we're going to have lunch now, but I'll call her tomorrow, okay?"

She barely had time to set the cat down and grab the kitchen towel to do a better job of wiping her cheeks before Sophie disconnected the video chat on her tablet and walked into the kitchen.

"Mommy, what's wrong? Do you have a cold?"

Her breath caught in her chest, and she closed her eyes against a fresh wave of pain. This was going to be hard. "Nothing, honey. Just a few sniffles. So

Cam has to go back to New York City for a while. We're going to take care of Elinor."

"Again?" Sophie rolled her eyes. "For how many days?"

"I'm not sure. Can you put more food in Oscar's bowl, honey? It's empty."

She wasn't ready to tell Sophie that Cam wouldn't be coming back this time. Her daughter would cry and maybe even cling to him, trying to keep him from going. It would be brutal for everybody. Maybe it would be easier to let him go, and then tell Sophie he was busy and couldn't come back yet. And Sophie would find other things to fill her time and maybe it wouldn't be such a big deal when Meredith finally had to tell her Cam was staying in the city.

It probably wasn't the healthy way to do it. But she wasn't sure how Cam would react to that kind of emotion from Sophie and he might say something that inadvertently hurt her even more. And Meredith knew she wasn't strong enough to get through a painful goodbye without breaking down. And if she broke down, so would Sophie.

Trembling, Meredith started the process of making lunch. Once she'd fed Oscar, Sophie pulled up a stool to help. They made tomato soup and grilled cheese sandwiches because Meredith wanted cooking and eating the meal to take long enough so Sophie wouldn't go running next door while she tried to regain some emotional equilibrium.

Meredith knew from experience that the trembling would fade away at some point. She could keep her chin up and make sure she has a smile on her face, but the hurt needed an outlet and the shaking that was imperceptible to others was her body's way of coping. It was a stress response she'd had since childhood, and there was nothing she could do about it.

Nothing but pretend she was okay while she waited to get over losing Cam.

Chapter Seventeen

Cam made two stops on his way out of Blackberry Bay. The first was at the office of Carolina's lawyer because he'd been dragging his feet on finalizing the estate. He hadn't been ready to make a final decision. But now it had been made for him.

He couldn't keep the cottage. Even if it was the sort of place his circle kept as summer homes, he couldn't drift in and out of Meredith's life. Seeing her on random weekends would only prolong the pain. He wouldn't see her enough to heal their relationship, but he'd see her enough to keep himself from moving on.

And there would come a weekend in the future

when he'd show up and there would be a man in the backyard, playing with Sophie and kissing Meredith. They both deserved that happy future, but Cam didn't want to be there to see it.

He was in the office for no more than fifteen minutes to give the man contact info for his assistant, who would be handling everything remotely going forward, except for the final signatures. They'd figure out how to handle that when the time came because he wasn't coming back.

"There will be crews going in to finish emptying it out," Cam said. "And then some minor updating. I want it in the paperwork that it can't be torn down. We'll find a seller who loves the cottage, who can also afford the taxes and upkeep."

"I don't specialize in real estate law, but I'm not sure you can dictate the buyer's intent after the purchase."

"Then we'll bluff, so at least we'll know the buyer doesn't have that intention when they sign the papers. I don't want it torn down."

The second stop was at the inn to pick up his mother, who'd actually hired a car service to bring her to town and then dismissed it, making it a one-way ride. She was so sure he would cave to her demands that she'd left herself no way home other than riding shotgun with him.

He drummed his fingers on the steering wheel

after sending her a text letting her know he was parked outside, letting his anger at her keep his pain down to a dull but persistent ache.

Maybe if things had gone differently with Meredith, he could have left his mother waiting at the inn until she finally surrendered and recalled the car service. But without Meredith, there was nothing to keep him here.

He hadn't been able to say goodbye. Meredith had made it pretty clear she didn't have anything else to say to him. And just the thought of Sophie's tears had made him unable to cross the lawn to her yard. Once everything of importance to him was loaded into his car, he'd seen Elinor curled up in Meredith's kitchen windowsill and realized he wouldn't even get that goodbye.

At some point he would probably call Tess Weaver, he told himself. She'd been kind to him and he should have seen her again before leaving Blackberry Bay. There were a lot of things he would regret about leaving today, but hurting Meredith and Sophie would be the thing that haunted him forever.

When his mother stepped out onto the sidewalk, his manners overrode his attitude and he got out to take her leather tote. His belongings filled the trunk and a good part of the back seat, but there was space behind his seat for it. Once she'd gotten into the passenger seat, he closed her door and took a long, slow breath.

It was going to be a very unpleasant drive back to the city.

Cam slowed as they neared the white sign with *Thank You for Visiting Blackberry Bay* written on it in fancy script letters.

He could turn around. He could drop his mother back at the inn before driving to Meredith's house and… What? What could he do? Ask her to leave behind the new life she's made for herself and daughter to move to the city? To uproot Sophie and bring her back into an environment where she'd be overwhelmed and have trouble making friends? Did he think he could ask them to start all over again in New York, where they'd wait night after night for him to get home from work?

No. They'd been through a lot and they were happy—truly happy—and he didn't want to put Meredith in the position of having to choose between a life with him and what was best for her daughter.

He accelerated past the sign and then glanced up at the moment it disappeared from his rearview mirror.

"There's nothing left for you back there," his mother said in an uncharacteristically soft voice. "The only thing you get from looking back is pain."

Then she went through the steps to sync her phone

with his car and he didn't object when she hit a button and an audiobook started playing through the speakers. It was some kind of cozy mystery, which surprised him. He hadn't realized his mother read for pleasure, and not having known that just added to the sadness clouding his mind.

Listening to the book kept either of them from feeling the need to make conversation, so by the time the five-hour drive was over and Cam navigated Manhattan and pulled his car into the underground parking garage that serviced the Maguire offices, they'd barely said a dozen words to each other.

He left everything but his wallet and phone locked in the car and rode the elevator up with his mother. Despite it being late evening, the offices were still bustling and some of the staff gave him questioning looks, as if they'd never seen a man in khaki shorts and a T-shirt before. Not a Maguire, anyway.

The door to his father's office was standing open, which meant security had probably told him his son was on his way up, but he paused when his mother stopped in the hallway.

"I'm going to go freshen up," she told him. "Shall I schedule a dinner for this weekend?"

"Sure." He didn't really care one way or another. He'd have to eat and, if it couldn't be Meredith, he didn't particularly care who he ate with.

Maybe it was because he was already at as low

an emotional point as he'd ever been, but walking into his father's office hit him harder than he expected. Calvin III looked up when he entered, and he was surprised to see some compassion in the older man's eyes.

"You're back."

"I am." He sat down in one of the leather armchairs, across from his father.

"Did you take care of everything you needed to take care of?"

The question was heavy with subtext and Cam sighed. There was a part of him that just wanted to blow the lid off everything. All three of them now knew the truth and not discussing it was ridiculous.

But his father—the man who *had* given him everything it was possible for him to give, even if he wasn't capable of offering love—was a proud man who was notoriously bad at discussing personal issues. Talking about Michael Archambault—about the time his wife had run off with another man and come back pregnant—wouldn't do anything but reopen old wounds.

Cam had what he needed. He had Carolina's journals, safely packed in a bag in the trunk of his car because he hadn't been able to leave them behind. He knew what truths there were to know, and one of those truths was that the man sitting in front of him was always going to be his father.

He was never going to be the kind of dad who inspired coffee mugs and Father's Day cards, but if Cam dug deep, there were moments. His father's hand squeezing his eighteen-year-old shoulder as he introduced him at a meeting as the future of the company. The way he'd stop what he was doing and make eye contact when congratulating Cam for a success—something he didn't bother doing with the majority of his people.

And on a more practical note—which would probably meet Calvin III's approval, which was ironic—if he turned his back on his father, he'd be walking away from the company, too. He'd invested too much of himself into it, and while he knew he could go off and build a company of his own, he didn't want to start over. His parents had made decisions that put his name on the letterhead, he'd worked hard to live up to the expectations and even exceeded them, and he wasn't giving it up.

"I did," he finally said. "There's nothing left for me there and I'm ready to get back to work."

"Good."

With a satisfied nod, his father cleared his throat and started talking about a potential merger on the horizon between two companies that, combined, could be competition for them.

Cam didn't listen. Everything being said was already in a report waiting in Cam's email inbox, and pain was obliterating his ability to focus.

There's nothing left for me there.

It hurt more than he'd believed it was possible to not only say those words, but to know they were true. He'd hurt Meredith by letting her believe what was happening between them was weakening his resolve to return to the city. Maybe he hadn't made her any promises, but he'd known Meredith and Sophie were both growing attached to him and he'd done nothing to stop it.

That somehow he could have them in his life and everybody could be happy was a lie he'd allowed himself to believe, and now they all were paying the price.

"I hate when it's raining," Sophie said, her voice a whine that grated across Meredith's raw nerves.

"Me, too," she said, even though it wasn't true in this moment, since the dark day matched her mood.

It also made her aware of how far Sophie had come. There was a time she wouldn't have minded the rain because all she wanted to do was stay in her room with her books all day. She still had a book with her, more often than not, but the book accompanied her outside and to the park and all sorts of adventures.

So moving to Blackberry Bay had done exactly

what Meredith had hoped. Her hometown had helped Sophie open up again and embrace her new community. She loved school and the library, and Kiki was still her best friend.

Meredith just wished it hadn't also come with a broken heart.

At least the rain keeping them inside meant she didn't have to watch the people who'd been in and out of the cottage for the last two weeks. It was empty now. She'd heard one of them say that, and later that evening, after everybody had left, she went and looked in through the slider. It looked lonely, sitting empty, and when Elinor made a mewling sound from next to her feet, she'd picked her and carried her back to her house, where she sat and cuddled the cat while she tried not to cry.

Tonight, she was going out. Reyna had insisted and, when Meredith had declined, she'd kept insisting until she'd finally asked her mother to take Sophie and Oscar for a night. Maybe it would do her good to get out of the house, but as she locked up and got into her car, all she wanted to do was crawl into bed and pull the covers over her head.

Putting on a brave face for Sophie had been all too familiar and, though not as hard as the days after Devin died, her little girl was as brokenhearted as she was. No matter how Meredith tried to explain that Cam had to go back to New York City for a work emergency and he was too busy to come back, she couldn't understand why her friend had just left like that and wouldn't be coming back. And she'd declared she already hated whoever their new neighbors were going to be.

Once she'd found a parking space, though, she tried her best to shake off the pain of the last two weeks, and by the time she spotted Reyna waiting at a table on the deck, she even managed to smile.

"Oh, honey, you look like you need a drink," her friend said, so apparently she hadn't done quite as good a job at smiling as she thought.

"Just one, since, unlike you, I have to drive home."

"Here's a better plan. We'll have dinner and one drink, and then we'll walk to my place, raid the bakery and then go upstairs to eat all of the cupcakes and drink until we fall asleep."

Meredith's laugh was genuine and much needed. "That sounds like a great plan if the goal is to be really sick tomorrow."

Reyna shrugged. "Okay, so maybe not *all* of the cupcakes."

After they'd ordered burgers and cocktails, Meredith braced herself for the question she knew was coming. She'd exchanged a few text messages with Reyna since Cam left, so her friend knew most of the story already, but the auto shop got busy with people waiting until the last minute to get their vehicles ready for the end-of-the-month inspection deadline, so it had been a few days since they'd spoken.

"Have you heard from him?"

Even though she'd known the question was coming, it still hurt. "No. And I don't expect to. If he was going to contact me, he would have done it by now."

Reyna scowled. "I don't get it. I mean, you guys were so obviously into each other and then he just leaves and that's it?"

"That's it." Her throat tightened and Meredith forced herself to take a deep breath. The last thing she was going to do was cry in this restaurant. "He has this whole life in New York City with power and money and the family business. Being here was like a time-out. And I knew it, and you knew it. Him leaving was not a surprise."

"But leaving the way he did was a jerk move." Reyna gave her a sad look. "And, honestly, I thought he'd change his mind."

So did I. "That's a lot to give up to live here in Blackberry Bay."

"You and Sophie are totally worth it, though."

That did it. Tears blurred Meredith's vision and no amount of blinking would hold them back. She used her napkin to blot at her eyes for a few seconds, trying to get her emotions under control before she turned into a spectacle.

"I'm sorry," Reyna said. "Let's talk about something else."

Meredith sniffed. "How's caramel apple guy?"

Reyna sighed. "He's still around. I like him, actually, and we've seen each other a few times."

"Maybe your bad-luck streak is coming to an end?"

"Maybe, but it's too soon to tell. You know what they say."

"That Reyna is hell on men," they said together.

They ate their burgers and Meredith nursed her cocktail, making sure to drink her water in between sips. Reyna noticed and reminded her of the cupcake-and-booze invitation, but she was going to pass. While getting out of the house had been good for her, what she really wanted to do was take a long, hot shower and then curl up in her bed and try to sleep.

"When you're ready, tell me and I'll get some ladies together and we'll have a true girls' night out," Reyna said after they'd finished and were out on the sidewalk. "I know you're not there yet, but meeting more people and reconnecting with more old friends will help cheer you up."

"Thanks. And thanks for tonight, too. It helped to get out and laugh a bit."

"Promise me you're not going to go home and cry yourself to sleep now."

"I promise." She'd stopped doing that a few nights

after Cam left and the numbness set in. She was so exhausted by getting herself and Sophie through each day that she fell asleep shortly after her head hit the pillow.

And she kept the promise. Mostly. By the time she crawled into bed and Elinor had nestled next to her feet, she didn't have any more tears to shed. She'd cried them all in the shower.

Chapter Eighteen

Cam had never realized his apartment was cold until now. It was professionally decorated, of course, but even with a color scheme of warm neutrals and throw pillows on the leather sofas, it felt barren and unwelcoming. Almost clinical, as though he was in a hospital waiting room, waiting to resume his regularly scheduled life.

In a way, he supposed he was. His time in Blackberry Bay had been nothing but a brief interlude, and he'd come away from the summer with nothing but an understanding of two people he hadn't known existed and could never meet.

And love for a woman and a little girl he'd walked away from.

He went through the motions every day. He'd get up after a restless night, shower and shave and then put on a suit. He went to the office. He did his job. He said the right things. He ate meals at mealtime and went to bed when the clock told him it was bedtime. But he was just an empty shell, moving through life on muscle memory and routine habits.

It was two weeks after his return that his mother showed up at his apartment unannounced after work, which was unusual in itself. But the softening in her eyes when he opened the door and saw his face told him something was very wrong.

"Is Dad okay?" he asked, trying to imagine what worst-case scenario had brought her to his door.

"He's the same as he always is. Can I come in for a minute? I'd like to have that talk now."

"I'm not really in the mood, to be honest."

"That woman—Meredith, I think her name was?" He nodded, hearing her name like a blow to his gut. "She was more than just your neighbor."

He turned away, not caring if she followed him in or turned around and left. He didn't even care if she closed the door behind her. He just didn't want to talk about Meredith. Yes, they'd been a lot more than neighbors. But it was over now.

Dropping on the couch, he rested his head against

the cushion and waited for her to get annoyed, say something harsh and leave. Rather than take the hint, though, his mom sat next to him and cleared her throat.

"I loved Michael." The words dropped like a stone between them, and Cam's brain scrambled for something to say as the seconds ticked away. Then his mom gave him a sad smile. "I don't know why, but I think it's important to tell you that. I loved him and we were happy, and then…"

Cam knew the *and then*. "You got pregnant with me."

"When it was just the two of us, learning to live without the advantages I'd always had felt like an adventure. You know how your father is. When I walked out on him, he made sure I knew I'd get nothing from him, and I was okay with that. I had Michael and we'd be fine. But once we knew there was a baby on the way, the stress of how we were going to pay not only for medical expenses, but diapers and all the things a baby needs started taking a toll. I didn't want to live that way, and I didn't want my baby to live that way."

"Did Dad know from the very beginning?"

Her lips pressed tightly together for a few seconds before she gave a sharp nod. "Yes. He knew I was pregnant when I came home because I told him immediately. We'd been trying to have a child for quite some time and he was under a lot of pressure from *his* father, so he benefited, as well. When we found out I was carrying a boy, the legal paperwork was handled. Calvin said it was never to be discussed again and that was the end of it."

"That sounds like Dad. All business."

"Yes, there was very little emotion in it. Unlike Michael, who was so excited when I told him I was expecting his baby. The expense and the stress... None of that mattered to him." Her stoic mask slipped even more, and he saw pain in her expression, still raw after all these years. "It was the hardest decision I ever had to make and maybe if Michael had fought—if he'd refused the money—I would have gone back to him. But he accepted the check and let me walk away forever."

"Mom." He hesitated, a part of him wanting to withhold information from her just as she'd withheld so much from him. But he thought of his grandmother and realized he didn't have it in him anymore to let somebody else suffer. "Carolina was a breast cancer survivor. She was diagnosed shortly after her son met you, based on her journal."

"What are you saying?"

"He told her he won big on a scratch ticket. He probably thought she would rather have drowned in medical debt or even lost the fight than have him give me up and, based on what I know about her now, he was right." His mother was shaking, and he covered her hand with his. "It probably doesn't help now, but he gave you—and his unborn child—up to save his mother."

"All these years, I thought he chose the money... just because." A tear slipped down her cheek. "Because people always choose the money. I did."

"You chose me," he said quietly, and he felt the hard ball of resentment dissolve as his heart made the decision to forgive her. Carolina would be so proud of him, he thought. "You were scared, with a baby coming, and I grew up in this amazing and privileged life. It's not an easy life to walk away from, I'm sure, especially if you're going to have a child to take care of."

"When I saw his picture on the wall of that cottage, it honestly felt as if somebody had reached into my chest and was squeezing my heart." She looked him in the eye. "I'm going to say this one time and I will never say it again, and you can learn from it what you will—I chose wrong."

She got up and walked out before he could even wrap his head around his mother's confession, never mind respond to it.

Her words stayed with him for the remainder of the night, confusing and unsettling him. *Learn from it what you will.* But when he stripped off his clothes and climbed into bed for another night of staring at the ceiling, it was Carolina's words that he couldn't get out of his head.

He just needs to know he can quit if he wants to.

"Cam!"

For a moment, Meredith thought she was imagining her daughter's joyful shout. That it was some random and painful memory from the summer echoing through her mind.

But then she saw Sophie streaking across the yard, Oscar at her heels, and her heart hammered in her chest as her hands balled into fists at her sides. Cam was actually here.

She didn't want to see him. He probably had paperwork to sign for the estate or some other business and then he'd be gone again. She wasn't sure she could take saying goodbye a second time, and she was tempted to barricade herself in her bedroom until he left. But there was Sophie to consider. Meredith wasn't the only passenger on this emotional roller coaster.

Moving to the window, she spotted Cam just in time to watch him crouch down and gather Sophie in his arms. He buried his face in her daughter's hair for a moment, but before Meredith could even catch her breath, his head lifted and his gaze locked onto her.

Sophie wasn't letting go, so as he pushed himself to his feet, he wrapped his arms around her and carried her across the yard. Meredith turned away, knowing she had only a short moment to get her emotions under control.

Elinor jumped up on the counter, which she wasn't supposed to do, and made a few chirping sounds.

"I know," Meredith said. "I saw him. What do you think he wants?"

The cat only tilted her head, and then turned when the slider opened. Elinor jumped down and walked away as if she couldn't be bothered with the man, and Meredith envied her the ability to do that.

But as soon as they got inside, Sophie lifted her head from Cam's shoulder. "Mommy, look! Cam came back. I told you he would."

Because her throat had tightened up when Cam stepped into her house, Meredith simply waited. This was where he would tell Sophie he was in Blackberry Bay for only a couple of days to sign some papers, or to do whatever it was he'd come back for. And she'd watch Sophie's heart break all over again, along with her own.

But he just set Sophie onto her feet. "Why don't you go play ball with Oscar for a little bit so I can talk to your mom?"

"No. I want to stay with you."

"Sophie Grace," Meredith said, her voice cracking slightly. "Just for a few minutes."

"I want to stay with Cam," she whined. "What if he leaves again?"

"I'll come play with you in a few minutes," Cam promised in soft voice. "I want to hear all about how school is going, okay?"

Very reluctantly, Sophie walked to the slider and pulled it open. Oscar went with her, and Elinor passed close enough to Cam to leave hair on his pants before she followed the others out. After giving Cam the saddest look she could muster, Sophie pulled the slider closed and sat on the deck to sulk.

Alone in her kitchen with Cam, Meredith heard nothing but the sound of her own breathing and the ticking of the analog clock she'd bought so Sophie could learn to tell time properly.

She'd noticed he hadn't promised Sophie he wouldn't leave again. Just that he'd play with her and hear about her new school.

"How long are you in town for?" she asked, deciding that facing the heartbreak head-on was the best way to go.

"I don't know yet." She winced and held up her hand as he took a step toward her. "I'm hoping Blackberry Bay will be my permanent address soon."

"You're going to stay here?" The only thing more painful than not seeing Cam would be randomly running into him at the market.

"I hope so."

"What about your job?"

"Things change."

She frowned, trying to make sense of the few words he was giving her. "Tell me you didn't walk away from everything—from a business that's been in the family for generations. And before you say it, yes, I remember that Calvin Maguire III is not your biological father, but he *is* your father."

"I didn't walk away. But I set some boundaries that are nonnegotiable. I'm going to continue to work remotely. Video chatting. Phone calls. Email. There's absolutely no reason I have to be physically in the office on a daily basis. There are times I *will* have to be there, so I'll keep my apartment and travel into the city when necessary."

Her heart was hammering in her chest, and she pressed her fingernails into her palm to give her something to focus on besides the hope trying to rise up inside her. "Having seen your mother in action, if only for a couple of minutes, I'm surprised your parents accepted that."

His jaw flexed. "I didn't give them a choice. When you're willing to walk away from the table for good and the other side knows it, you have a lot more power."

"So why did you come back here, Cam?"

"Because there's no place else I want to be." His jaw clenched as he swallowed hard. "I want to make a life with you here in Blackberry Bay, together. I love you, Meredith. I want to spend the rest of my life with you. And Sophie's not my daughter, but I love that little girl."

"Even when she's a teenager and only looks up from her phone long enough to tell me she hates me?" she asked, trying to inject enough humor to keep herself from bursting into tears.

"Even then." He cleared his throat. "But this is about you and me, Meredith."

"I'm a mother. Nothing is ever just about me. You broke that little girl's heart. You didn't even say goodbye to her."

"I couldn't." He pressed his lips together and blinked a couple of times before clearing his throat. "I'm sorry I did that. I always will be, but I wasn't strong enough to say goodbye to her."

She understood that, even if it would be hard to forgive him for it. "I kept telling her you were busy and then finally told her you were too busy to come back. Even though she missed you so much she'd cry, she believed the whole time that you *would* come back."

"I'm here, and if you'll have me, I'll never leave either of you again. I want to be all in. I want to go to sleep with you in my arms and wake up to your hair tickling my nose. I want to celebrate your wins and hold you through your losses and everything in between."

"I want that, too. So much. I do." She swallowed hard past the lump in her throat. "But you have to be sure. If you go out there and tell that little girl you're staying and you leave again? And me. If you tell me you're staying, you have to stay, Cam. Forever."

"Do you love me, Meredith?"

"Yes," she whispered. "Completely."

"You know I have baggage. I learned a lot about who I could have been while I was here, and I hope that knowledge will change who I actually am for the better, but I'll always be a Maguire. I mean, you met my mother. That was a particularly ugly version of her, but she's not exactly the warm and fuzzy type even on her best day. Not even Christmas."

She laughed through her tears. "I'll make a note to spend Christmases with *my* parents."

"Yes." He sucked in a breath and stared at the ceiling for a long moment before walking slowly toward her. "I can see it, Meredith. Waking up with you in my arms on Christmas morning. Sophie running in and jumping on the bed because she wants to open her presents."

"I can see it, too," she said, stepping into his arms.

"Will you marry me?"

She gazed up into his blue eyes and saw his love

for her—his certainty—shining there. "Yes. Yes, I'll marry you."

He lifted her off her feet and kissed her so hard it took her breath away. The weeks apart and the tears were all but forgotten as she wrapped her arms around him and held him close.

It was the high-pitched squeal that finally broke up the kiss. As Cam set her on her feet, she turned to see Sophie staring at them. She was clapping and bouncing up and down on her toes, with a yipping Oscar on one side of her and Elinor on the other.

"Our family is excited for us," she said, looping her arm around his waist.

"I'm not sure about the cat, actually." He kissed the top of her head. "But I love the sound of that. *Our* family."

Epilogue

"How do you think Carolina would feel about this?"

Meredith heard the emotion in Cam's voice and wrapped her arms around his waist. "I think she'd love it."

They were standing in the middle of the cottage, but it was almost unrecognizable. The renovation had been extensive, right down to the studs, and now the interior was bright and airy, with light hardwood floors and new furnishings.

Movement outside the newly replaced glass sliding door caught her eye and she saw Elinor pacing out on the deck, pausing with each pass to glare at them. During the renovations, they'd removed the cat door and she was highly displeased.

"I don't think Elinor loves it, though," she murmured.

Cam laughed. "She'll get used to it. But we should probably put a note in the rental listing letting people know there will be a bossy cat trying to visit them."

"The bus will be here soon," Meredith said after a glance at her watch. "We should finish up."

"It doesn't *feel* like Carolina's cottage." Her fiancé clearly wasn't ready to leave yet.

"It will, when people are staying here, laughing and relaxing and making summer memories together." She took his hand and tugged him toward the door—not the slider, but the new front door with the electronic keypad. "Come on."

When they were standing in the front yard, she felt his hand relax in hers. The inside of the cottage might be all new, but outside, it was all Carolina. They'd freshened up the pink paint. The trim and window boxes had a fresh coat of turquoise and, though they'd straightened all the window boxes, they'd left some of the plastic flowers.

Every touch that they could tell had been Carolina's had been repaired and repainted and touched up, so it had eclectic and adorable curb appeal, while keeping the heart she had poured into it.

And next to the door was a small sign Sophie and

Meredith had painted, with *Welcome to Carolina's Cottage* in a carefully written childish script.

"You're right," Cam said. "She'd love this."

They heard the bus coming up the road and a few seconds later, Oscar ran toward them from the backyard. He stopped a few feet shy of the road, his little body shaking with excitement, while the bus stopped and Sophie climbed down the big steps.

After waving to her friends on the bus as it pulled away, she hugged her dog and then hugged Meredith before turning to Cam. She put her arms up and he lifted her off her feet for a big hug—he loved hugs—before setting her back on her feet.

"How was school today?" he asked, taking her backpack as they walked down the driveway.

But Meredith saw the way he looked back at the cottage as they walked, his mouth curving into a soft smile that warmed her heart.

Keeping the cottage had been the right decision. They'd talked through all of their options and eventually Cam had been able to say he didn't care what made financial sense. He wanted to keep it and fix it up without stripping it of everything that made it special.

They'd considered making it his office, since he'd need space for more than his laptop. He needed a proper desk and a printer and a setup for video meetings and all of the other clutter an office needed. But he wanted more separation between his work and his family, so he'd rented a private office space in town and they'd decided to make the cottage a short-term rental so other families could enjoy the lake during the summer.

"There's only one more month until summer vacation," she heard Sophie telling Cam as they went in the house to go through the after-school routine of emptying her backpack and doing her homework.

At least one day during the week, he made sure to wrap up at his office and be home in time to meet the bus, and then he'd work on his laptop at the table while Sophie did her homework and Meredith started getting dinner ready. He'd taken today off to do a final walk-through of the cottage with the contractor before cutting the last check.

After dinner came Meredith's favorite part of the day. It still got chilly as the sun got low in the sky, so they grabbed a blanket and went to the backyard.

She had no idea where Cam had found it, but one day she'd come home from volunteering at the senior center to find a huge, double-wide hammock on a stand in the backyard. It had taken them a few tries to master it, but now Meredith and Cam were able to get in and then steady it while Sophie climbed in between them. Last up was Oscar, while Elinor stretched out on the deck rail and watched them all.

Looking out over the still water of Blackberry Bay, Meredith listened to Sophie and Cam talking about what kind of ice cream they were going to get when their favorite ice-cream parlor opened for the Memorial Day weekend.

Turning her head, she met Cam's gaze and smiled. He arched one eyebrow, questioning, and she nodded. It was time.

"Mommy and I have some fun news," he said to Sophie. Then he glanced back at Meredith, leaving it to her.

She kissed the top of her daughter's head. "How do you feel about having a baby brother or sister?"

Sophie managed to jab each of them several times with her little elbows as she sat up. "A baby? I love babies!"

Meredith laughed because Sophie didn't actually know many babies, but as long as her daughter was happy, so was she. "Yes, a new baby."

Sophie flopped back down between them and heaved a very dramatic sigh.

"What's the sigh for?" Cam asked gently, reaching his hand across his body to ruffle her hair.

"We're going to need a bigger hammock."

As Cam's laughter filled the yard, with Sophie's high-pitched giggle joining in, Meredith's heart swelled with love and she closed her eyes. She'd come home to Blackberry Bay looking for happiness.

She'd found love.

* * * * *